The Best of
The First Line
The First Three Years

Edited by
David LaBounty and Jeff Adams

Blue Cubicle Press
2003

Published by
Blue Cubicle Press, LLC
P.O. Box 250382
Plano, TX 75025-0382

© 2003 by Blue Cubicle Press, LLC. All rights reserved.
Printed in the United States of America.

No part of this book may be reproduced, stored in a retrieval system, or transmitted, in any form or by any means, except for inclusion of brief quotations in a review, without permission in writing from the publisher.

All of the stories appearing in this book were first published in *The First Line*.

ISSN 1525-9382
ISBN 0-9745900-0-2

LIBRARY OF CONGRESS CATALOG CARD NUMBER: 2003113359

First Printing: November 2003

137 11 3 150

Contents

Introduction   i

VOLUME 1 ISSUE 1:   *Just like his fifth grade teacher, Mr. Young, had always told him, Brian put on his thinking cap.*

   Jennifer Bass. *Vacation*   3
   Harold Brown. *What's Red and Blue and Green All Over?*   5
   Theo Glenn. *End of the Line*   7

VOLUME 1 ISSUE 2:   *The rules are clearly spelled out in the brochure.*

   Joe Austin. *Beautiful Shoulders*   11
   Bruce Standley. *Food, Glorious Food*   13
   Larry M. Keeton. *Rules*   15

VOLUME 1 ISSUE 3:   *"Well, there's ten minutes of my life I'll never get back."*

   W. Eric Martin. *Revised Text for Fourth Quarter Advertisement*   21
   Lara Kenney. *Nothing of Value*   23
   Kathleen Crow. *Lessons*   25

VOLUME 1 ISSUE 4:   *As the curtain rose, the scenario began to play itself out.*

   David LaBounty. *Exit, Stage Left*   29
   Ed Phelts. *A Tale Told by an Idiot*   31
   Matt Miller. *The Recital*   33

VOLUME 2 ISSUE 1: *The picture told the entire story.*

Clifford Turner. *Tavern Clown* 37
Richard Lee Zuras. *A Photo of my Dad* 39
Chris Buchan. *The Locket* 41

VOLUME 2 ISSUE 2: *The person on the train kept saying, "I believe," over and over and over.*

Joseph Horne. *Train* 45
Lisa Firke. *Winging It* 47
Walter Addison March. *On the Bubble* 49

VOLUME 2 ISSUE 3: *My father and I left on a Thursday.*

Greg Wahl. *Under a Zorro Moon* 53
Kristine Coblentz. *The Goats of Heaven* 55
Tracie Clayton. *Hold the Cards and Flowers* 57

VOLUME 2 ISSUE 4: *I remember the radio was playing the best song.*

Josh Beddingfield. *I Fought 3 a.m. and Won: Kurt Weil vs. Outdoor Lighting* 61
Kim Perrone. *A Window to the Soul* 63
Spencer Williams. *The Lingering Death of My Electric Dream* 65

VOLUME 2 ISSUE 5: *Whitney Heather Yates knew she was in trouble from the moment she learned how to spell her name.*

E. Catherine Tobler. *The Writing on the Wall* 71
Mary Kay Lane. *Saying Yates* 73
Mari Whyte. *"Why?"* 75

VOLUME 2 ISSUE 6: *It sounded like she said, "Every day when I get home, I find a naked body in the bed."*

   Hester Eastman. *Just Making Conversation*   81
   Sharon O'Hara. *For Entertainment Purposes Only*   83
   Joshua McDonald. *The First Day*   85

VOLUME 3 ISSUE 1: *"It was the only thing he couldn't do for her."*

   Miranda Garza. *Through the Eyes of Revenge*   89
   Nick Aires. *The Bonda Prophecy*   91
   Ben Lareau. *Only Things*   93

VOLUME 3 ISSUE 2: *The party was only the beginning of what would happen tonight.*

   Kelli A. Wilkins. *Guest of Honor*   97
   Ehren Hemet Pflugfelder. *The Distance Between People*   99
   John Tennel. *Picture Imperfect*   101

VOLUME 3 ISSUE 3: *Hal couldn't sleep.*

   Chris Salter. *The Box*   105
   Joy L. McDowell. *Cutting Losses*   107
   Michael Kelly. *Learning to Fly*   109

VOLUME 3 ISSUE 4: *"Step this way as our tour of Earth continues."*

   Dick Brown. *Atlas*   113
   Dale Thomas Smith. *Earth Follies*   115
   Melissa Mead. *Worlds Apart*   117

VOLUME 3 ISSUE 5: *"Please state your name for the court."*

Jeff Adams. *Television Trials*   121
Jennifer Schwabach. *Queen for a Day*   123
Simon Wood. *Your Name, Please*   125

VOLUME 3 ISSUE 6: *"How did you end up with a nickname like that?"*

Margaret B. Davidson. *An Arrangement of Convenience*   129
T. K. Harris. *The Nickname*   132
G. W. Thomas. *Lazarus*   133

Contributors   135

Introduction

It all starts the same but...

The idea for *The First Line* originated over twelve years ago with a visit to Washington D.C. I was in the city for a Construction Writers' Association conference and to visit my friends from college, Robin and David. We were driving down K Street, when Robin, always the instigator, prodded us to write somthing together. I suggested we end each letter with a sentence that the other had to use to write a story that would accompany the next letter. (These were the pre-email days, so our correspondences were lengthy letters that contained puzzles, chess moves, and of course, stories.) I got the idea from one of my favorite movies, *Out of Africa*. David agreed the idea would be fun. To make it more challenging though, he suggested the stories couldn't be longer than one page.

Over the next several years, sentences were sent back and forth across the country. (I would eventually move to northern California, while Robin and David would end up in Montana.) Some of the stories inspired by our first lines were good; some of them were terrible. Some of them were less than a page; some needed a little creative desktop publishing in order to keep the words from spilling over. Some stories even turned out to be the seeds for longer tales that were eventually published.

The stories stopped in 1995, as did the letters. E-mail had reared its wonderfully ugly head, and communication became easier, cheaper, and not quite as creative.

The years passed. I got married and moved to New York. David and Robin headed to Idaho for graduate school and then found themselves in Texas.

One night, I got a call from David. He and Robin had come up with this idea for a magazine based on our literary game: we provide the sentences and invite other writers to send us their stories. It sounded like fun, so I signed on.

Those of you who've been here from the beginning know that we started thin. The first three years, the best of which you are holding, we refer to as "the flat years." Those were the days when the magazine was four sheets (five if we were lucky) of 8 1/2 by 14 inch paper folded and stapled. Each story was limited to 800 words, keeping with our original one-page premise.

Some great stories came out of those first three years, and whittling them down for this anthology wasn't easy. It took us three months to read everything and settle on a story list. David and I provided all but two of the sentences in this anthology. The sentences for Volume 2 Issue 6 and Volume 3 Issue 1 were Lisa Firke's and Pamela Garza's respectively. Lisa won our first First Line contest, and Pamela was the runner-up (having been the readers' favorite).

You don't get rich running a literary magazine; but if you're lucky, you can break even and have the creativity at least pay for itself. That's what *The First Line* has done almost from the beginning. We've got a lot of devoted writers and readers to thank for that. We've truly grown by word of mouth—through writer's groups, college classes, and some great reviews. We don't know what the future holds, but as long as we continue to have fun, we'll continue to print the best stories that spring from the same first line.

Jeff

Volume 1 Issue 1

Just like his fifth grade teacher, Mr. Young, had always told him, Brian put on his thinking cap.

Jennifer Bass

Vacation

Just like his fifth grade teacher, Mr. Young, had always told him, Brian put on his thinking cap.

Slipping the cold metal over his bald head and ears, he tightened the purple chin-strap, picked up the remote control, and pressed the soft, red button marked ON. He knew the tingling sensation meant that thousands of wiry, hair-like electrodes were wriggling through flesh, drilling through bone, then attaching to various spots of brain tissue. Within seconds, it was working.

Brian questioned himself, "What should I get Mother for her eightieth birthday?"

He answered himself, "A bottle of perfume or an all-expenses-paid trip to New Pennsylvania."

A trip to New Pennsylvania? Last he heard, the Amish riots were still raging out of control. In fact, weren't some cities still burning? He asked himself, "What kind of perfume?"

He replied, "A trip to New Pennsylvania."

Brian raised an eyebrow and paused. What had he meant by that? He again questioned, "What kind of *perfume*?"

He again answered, "A trip to New Pennsylvania."

Brian gave the metallic cap a few whacks before trying once more.

Same thing. New Pennsylvania.

Puzzled, he examined the underside of the remote. Nothing seemed loose, so he turned it back over and pressed the spongy square button marked RESET. A whirring noise above each ear, a buzz at the base of his cortex, and the machine was ready. He took a deep breath. "What should I buy Mother for her birthday?"

"An all-expenses-paid trip to New Pennsylvania."

Brian's face grew warm. Confused, and slightly agitated, he smacked the remote with the palm of his hand and banged the thinking cap with his fist. Syllable by syllable, with hefty pauses between each word, he asked, "What would Mother like for her birthday?"

Slowly, mockingly, he answered himself, "Send her on a vacation to New Pennsylvania."

"Argh!" Brian cried.

"Argh!" he cried back to himself.

Brian turned off the contraption and waited for the tingling sensation to cease before ripping the chin-strap, removing the cap, and drop-kicking the thing into a corner. He stood in the middle of the room and pointed an accusing finger at the dented metal crying, "Damn Mr. Young, and damn technology!"

For her eightieth birthday, Brian's mother received a small, lavender-colored crystal bottle of lilac perfume.

Harold Brown

What's Red and Blue and Green all Over?

Just like his fifth grade teacher, Mr. Young, had always told him, Brian put on his thinking cap.

"Well?"

"I'm thinking. I'm thinking." Brian scratched his head where the imaginary cap was sitting.

"It's not possible," Timmy said.

"Yes it is," Brian said annoyed, not as much at his friend, but at his own inability to come up with an answer. And he better—fast. His whole comic book collection was riding on this.

"Give it up," his friend said. "Superman is the strongest, smartest, best looking superhero around. No one can beat him."

"What about Spiderman?" Brian said, knowing Spiderman was no match for the Man of Steel. The look on Timmy's face confirmed that.

"You think a little webbing is going to stop Supe? Try again."

Brain shook his head. Batman was out. Sure he was smart and he had all sorts of cool gadgets, but even with Robin at his side, all Superman had to do is blow them into outer space with one puff of his super breath. Wonder Woman? She was a girl. The Hulk? He was strong, but dumb. Even the whole team of X-Men and women wouldn't be a match for Superman. Stupid mutants.

"Time's up! Hand over the comics."

"What about Doomsday?" Brian blurted out.

Timmy shook his head. "Not a superhero."

"Yeah, but he killed Superman."

"Yeah, but the bet was which superhero is better than Superman. Not which bad guy. Now quit stalling."

Brian looked down at his stack, defeated. It was a stupid bet. He knew no one was stronger than Superman. He only made the bet because of Timmy's bragging.

Brian handed over the first comic. On the cover, the Hulk was crushing an army tank under his feet. Big, stupid, green ape, Brian thought to himself.

"Come on," Timmy said, impatiently. "Hand 'em over."

Brian looked into the eyes of the green monster and smiled. "I know who can beat Superman with one finger," he said, confidently.

"You've already lost the bet," Timmy said.

"Come on. Double or nothing on your baseball cards?"

Timmy hesitated. "You're on," he said, cautiously. "Who?"

"The Green Lantern."

Timmy frowned. "No way. He's just a wuss with a magic ring."

And what color is his ring?" Brian asked.

"Green," Timmy said, as if his friend was an idiot. "So what's he going to do? Shoot green bullets at him?" Timmy laughed.

"And what's the only thing that can harm Superman?"

"Kryptonite," Timmy said slowly.

"And what color is Kryptonite?"

Timmy didn't answer.

"That's right," Brian said, taking his comic books back. "All the Green Lantern has to do is shoot some Kryptonite at Superman—from his green ring—and the Man of Steel is dead."

"But, but, but," Timmy stammered.

"Sorry, Bud. You lose. Superman was just beat by a wuss wearing a ring."

Theo Glenn

End of the Line

Just like his fifth grade teacher, Mr. Young, had always told him, Brian put on his thinking cap.

They weren't in his pants pockets or his jacket. "Now where the Hell did I put them?" Brian lifted up his plate, the napkin, the napkin holder—even the salt shaker. "Shit!"

The couple at the next table gave him a strange look.

Brain managed a small, apologetic smile and dropped to his knees. He felt around under the table where he found a partially dried puddle of pancake syrup. With his left hand stuck to the floor, Brian pressed down hard on his right hand, hoping to peel his sticky palm off the linoleum. Suddenly, there was a sharp pain in the palm of his right hand. He let out a little yelp and quickly pulled up both hands.

Brian sat back and looked at his palm. A piece of ceramic, left over from when the waitress dropped his coffee cup on the floor, was sticking out of his hand, right below his index finger. Brian watched as a small river of blood seeped out of the wound like a river of lava flowing from a recently erupted volcano.

"This is great. Just great," Brian muttered to himself.

Carefully, Brian pried the miniature dagger from its fleshy hilt and placed the wounded area in his mouth.

"What's the matter, Hon?"

Brian stopped sucking on his hand and looked up at the waitress. "Do you have a bandage?"

"Cut yourself?"

Brain nodded.

"Be right back."

Brian pulled himself back into his seat. He examined his hand. The bleeding had stopped, but there was a split in the skin where the shard had been.

Brian looked over his palm at the thousands of lines, crisscrossing in what looked like a road map: three main highways and hundreds of back streets. And that one, very small vertical line in the middle of it all. What was that line called? He never really thought about having his palm read before. But lately, everything seemed to be going wrong. Maybe the secrets to his life were coded in the lines of his hand. He had passed a place just down the road. A poorly painted sign outside a dilapidated house read: MADAM ZORINSKY: PALMIST. Maybe it was worth the ten bucks to find out.

"Here you go, Hon. What were you doin' on the ground?"

"Looking for my keys," Brian said.

"Did you try your pockets?"

Brian nodded.

"How 'bout the ignition?"

Brain's hope was short lived as he stepped out of the diner and into the hot desert air. It was gone. Unfortunately, the waitress was right.

Brian walked back into the diner, defeated. "Okay, everybody. If I could have your attention."

The diner quieted down and all eyes were on him.

"There's going to be a short delay."

There were a few groans and grumbles. Brian lifted his hand to try and appease them. "I'm sorry about the inconvenience. But the bus seems to have been stolen. I'll call Dispatch. They'll have a replacement here in no time."

The grumbles turned to shouts of 'What about our luggage!' and 'I'm going to be late!'

Brian's head was aching in rhythm with his palm. He went over to the pay phone in the corner, picked up the receiver, and paused. How was he going to explain losing this one?

Volume 1 Issue 2

The rules are clearly spelled out in the brochure.

Joe Austin

Beautiful Shoulders

The rules are clearly spelled out in the brochure.

1. All clothes must be checked in at the disrobing house just beyond the entry gate.
2. Every guest may acquire a terry-cloth wrap in exchange for their clothing. (Guests may supply their own. We only have sizes to 2XL.)
3. Terry-cloth Velcro waist wraps are not required at dining, but permitted.
4. No cameras or video recording devices allowed beyond the disrobing house.
5. All guests must be 25 years of age or older.
6. Enjoy your natural self.

It was the sixth rule of the Eden Acres Nudist Camp that made Beverly smile. It had been years since she felt that she had enjoyed her natural self. When she stopped to think about it, she couldn't remember if she actually once had enjoyed her natural self, or only believed that she had. Would several sexual partners in college count? No, she thought. That was cheap thrills. That was drunkenness. Now, as her thirtieth birthday approached, Beverly wanted to do something very different this June 3rd. She was surfing the Web and found the Eden Acres Nudist Camp and requested a brochure. That would be different. That could be just the rejuvenation she needed as she headed into her 30s, she thought.

Enjoy your natural self, huh? Beverly put the brochure down on the table and went to her bedroom. She took off her t-shirt and pulled down her shorts. She unhooked her bra and pulled her panties off. She wanted to see herself differently than she normally did. The only time she ever truly looked at herself naked was when she would step out of the shower, and, to be honest with herself, she was usually covered in a towel, even when she was home alone. Beverly touched her throat and then let her fingers run down her breasts and down her stomach. She touched the little line of blonde hair that ran from her navel around the curve of her little belly and down into her pubic hair. She turned halfway around and examined her ass. Okay, so she wasn't the most beautiful woman in the world. She was short with strong looking legs and hardly any knees at all. "Thanks, Mom," she said out loud. She looked at her ass again. At least it had a nice roundness to it. It was shaped like a Valentine's Day heart with a bit of plumpness where it mattered—at the place where it met her legs.

Next, she looked at her shoulders. Her mother had always told her she had beautiful shoulders. Her mother had told her that they would set her apart from other women in an instant. "You have starlet shoulders, Bev. Like the old Hollywood beauties," and her mother would touch them. "They jut right out, demanding attention. They frame your body beautifully. Christ, why couldn't I have gotten those shoulders."

Would her beautiful shoulders be enough to give her the confidence to spend a week at a nudist camp? Would she be able to play volleyball with men and women completely naked? Could she really, honestly, see herself sitting down to have drinks with new friends, some fat, some beautiful, all naked?

She touched her shoulders. They were outstanding shoulders. They really did nicely frame her short body. She walked, naked, to the kitchen, found the brochure, and called the phone number on the front. Looking at her kitchen calendar, she looked at the week of June 3rd to book a reservation. Who cares? she thought. I've got great shoulders.

Bruce Standley

Food, Glorious Food

The rules are clearly spelled out in the brochure. Each entrant had to devise his recipe using only Professor Patrick's Pickled Pork Products as the main ingredient.

"You've got to be kidding me!" bellowed Chef Bernard from behind his cooking battery. "And what am I supposed to do with brined pigs' feet? This is outrageous! I can't believe you dragged me all the way down here to this, this supposed gastronomic world series to create a masterpiece from, from… leftovers!!"

Bernard was on a rant again. Next to his culinary talents, it was the thing he did best. If he had known what he would be cooking, I never would have gotten him on the plane.

"No, Chef, you don't have to if you don't want to. I'm sure one of the other contestants will be happy to take home the $10,000 first prize."

"Well hold on there, let's not be too hasty. That could buy a lot of pigs' feet. Alright, what else is in that little basket of assorted goodies?"

"Of course there's pickled pigs' feet, pickled jowls, pickled ears, pickled tongues, pickled brains, pickled shanks—this looks good—spicy pickled snouts, and this one has the label missing, but it seems to be staring back at me."

"Fantastic, what else can we use?"

"There's a load of staples in the cupboard next to the range with fresh veggies and condiments. Remember, Professor Patrick's must be the main ingredient, and you only have one hour."

And with that, the buzzer sounded, and a flurry of activity set the wheels of pickled pork products in motion. A crowd had gathered on the main concourse to watch as thirty of the best chefs from around the world whipped up tasty creations. Sauté pans sizzled, deep fryers bubbled, woks stir fried in a frenzy all vying for bragging rights and a hefty paycheck. After sixty minutes, the buzzer once again sounded, and all the contestants presented some of the most unappealing food in the world in the most artistic and tasteful ways. The judges poked and prodded, tasted and savored. They gathered in a little huddle after each tasting and scribbled little notes. On down the line they went until they reached contestant number twenty seven. Chef Bernard.

Bernard had put a great deal of thought into his delicacy. Perhaps a full minute or two due to the surprise of the entire event. His dish, Kentucky Jowls in Bourbon with Wild Mushrooms and Fresh Sage was presented on a bed of fried endive and batter fried enoki mushrooms. He watched patiently as the judges made their way through his entree and deliberated amongst themselves, drawing conclusions on what Bernard had prepared.

"I think they like it," I whispered in his ear.

"I still can't believe you dragged me down here," he returned.

The judges breezed through the final three contestants. After a few more minutes of deliberation, the head judge stood.

"I would like to thank all of our tremendous contestants for the wonderful work they have done today. And now to present the award to the first place winner, I would like to introduce Professor Patrick himself."

Professor Patrick took the podium. "The first place finisher in this year's Professor Patrick's Pickled Pork Products competition is Son Yap for his Brains Teriyaki and Fried Rice Noodle. He will receive this beautiful plaque and $10,000 worth of Professor Patrick's Pickled Pork Products."

I never saw Chef Bernard after that. It's kind of funny how you don't read the fine print when someone mentions $10,000.

Larry M. Keeton

Rules

The rules are clearly spelled out in the brochure. How did I get myself into this quagmire?

Sitting in the wooden pew, waiting for my turn at judgment, I recalled the day I met him. Handsome devil, his presence commanded the room. His eyes gazed upon me. I blushed. The suit's thin white lines accentuated his power. The people flocked around him like pigeons to breadcrumbs. He raised his right arm and they fell back, clearing a path. His magnetism pulled me towards him. Slowly at first, and then picking up speed until I was within his aura.

"Your soul has a problem," he said.

"How'd you know?"

His lips parted, showing teeth of angel wing whiteness. "I sense these things."

"Sure."

"You're concerned about money for the baby and the flirtatious receptionist in your office. It's natural that you desire her. I can help."

"What's the catch?"

A royal blue brochure with fluffy white clouds appeared. He passed it to me. I read the crimson words. Finishing, I felt I had a chance.

"All you have to do is sign," he said. "And follow the rules set forth in the brochure."

"If I don't?"

"Your soul is sold to the highest bidder. Sometimes I win; sometimes I lose. Follow the rules, and we won't have a problem." He extended a gold pen towards me.

I signed. Life improved immediately. The secretary found another job. I made a killing in stocks. My marriage thrived. Our son was the town's football hero en route to Stanford University on an academic scholarship.

Then, she entered my life, a raven beauty with hypnotic eyes that set on me. It was only a matter of time before I succumbed. It was heavenly. But, the moment I finished, guilt swarmed through me like African killer bees in search of North America.

Per the rules, I witnessed the proceedings the day after my indiscretion. A black coated auctioneer called forth the brochures. The subject stood during the bidding process. On the right was the angel of eternal life, on the left, the demon of death. Today the demon had won most of the bids.

My brochure was called. I stood, my legs gelatin strong. The angel gave me a cursory glance and then checked a book before him.

"One thousand," the angel offered in the opening bid.

The demon tapped a computer keyboard and examined the screen. "Five thousand for this fine soul."

The angel perused the book's page. My heart beat rapidly, knowing I was a goner. Sweat felt like it was sizzling down my cheeks.

"Six thousand," the angel said.

"Ten thousand," the demon responded.

"Eleven."

"Fifteen."

My eyes widened as I watched the angel close the book. My heart thundered in my ears. I was sure my neighbor could hear it.

"I have a bid of fifteen thousand," the auctioneer said. "Going once." Long pause. "Going twice." An eternal pause.

"One hundred thousand," the angel said.

The people in the room let out a collective gasp.

"One hundred thousand is bid," the auctioneer stated, looking toward the demon.

The demon shook his head.

"SOLD!" and the slamming of a gavel reverberated throughout my body. I collapsed into my chair, my breathing rapid. A strong hand grasped my left shoulder. I turned to see the warm face of the man who had signed my brochure.

"I told you. Sometimes I win."

I grinned in renewed faith. "I believe in you."

"As you should," he said, "as you should. After all, forgiveness is my business."

———————

Volume 1 Issue 3

"Well, there's ten minutes of my life I'll never get back."

W. Eric Martin

Revised Text for Fourth Quarter Advertisement

"Well, there's ten minutes of my life I'll never get back."

Woman [Beverly, late thirties, subtly attractive, dinner party-style dress] stands at a kitchen sink, wearing rubber gloves, holding a plastic dish brush. The sink is filled with gray water. The dish rack is piled with dripping dishes and pots. Through a doorway, fifteen feet behind Beverly, are visible three men and two women, laughing and chatting in a living room setting. A woman walks through the doorway into the living room and closes the door, shutting off the laughter; Beverly sighs.

Voiceover: "That's what you think! With TimeCo's revolutionary new WhiskBack, you won't miss a moment of your next dinner party: the embarrassing stories told about friends who didn't show, the quiet sexual give-and-take with your next-door neighbor. You can have it all!"

Visual: Beverly goes from startled to a hint of understanding to a full satisfied smile accompanied by a head tilt.

Voiceover: "With the patented tachyon technology of WhiskBack, you can finally be in two places at once. Let's watch!"

Visual: Graphic of WhiskBack against swirling green and white background. Cartoony blue bubbles rise from the horns on the top and sides of the machine. Jagged word balloon [yellow type on blue background] under the machine reads:

"Tachyons = time to spare!"

Switch to Beverly, now holding WhiskBack. Move to headshot [camera to the side to keep her face and smile visible] as she places the horns under her chin, then the suction cup on her forehead.

Voiceover: "So easy to use, you'll be traveling back to the past in no time!"

Back to full body shot. Beverly, feet together, shoulders back, places the first two fingers of each hand through the trigger holes.

Voiceover: "It's set for ten minutes. Let's go!" Fade.

Switch to living room scene. View is from over the back of an empty chair, looking down a coffee table at a man in a similar chair [Tom, dark blond hair, clean shaven, black turtleneck shirt]; a couch on each side of the table holds a couple; the women hold coffee cups low in their laps. The man on the right-hand couch sits near the empty chair and holds a half-full wine glass; three more glasses sit on the table. The man on the left-hand couch sits close to Tom and is laughing at Tom's jokes; the other three talk to each other, but more quietly. A door is open on the room's back wall, and Beverly can be seen leaning over a counter, washing dishes.

Tom: "So I told him, if he's going to act that way—" [breaks off as Beverly enters the room and closes the door; before the door closes, Beverly can still be seen washing dishes in the kitchen] [Tom sounds puzzled] "Honey, I thought you were doing the dishes."

Beverly [circling around room]: "Oh, I will, dear. But I want to spend as much time as possible with our friends before the evening ends." As Beverly sits in the chair, the man to her right hands her a full glass of wine, winking.

Beverly turns to the camera: "I can't believe how much better my life has become since I bought the WhiskBack!" She turns back to the man on her right. The camera zooms in on the door as Beverly opens it from the kitchen. Still wearing rubber gloves, she gives a thumbs-up and a big smile through the crack in the door.

Freeze image. Superimpose logo on bottom third of screen. Voiceover: "Anytime you need more time is a great time for WhiskBack!"

Lara Kenney

Nothing of Value

"Well, there's ten minutes of my life I'll never get back." Deirdre opened the bottle of wine she had grabbed on the way out of his apartment. It was good wine, and his apartment—a restored loft in the old bankers' district—had been nicer than those of most men she went home with on Friday nights.

Her roommates laughed as she filled their empty glasses. "Ten minutes, you should feel lucky," one of them said, "last week my guy passed out before he had his pants unbuttoned." Along with the wine, Deirdre had snatched a box of candlesticks, a round of brie, and an unopened tube of toothpaste she found in the medicine chest. This was their late night Friday routine: the five of them together in the living room, laughing about the men they had slept with that night and rooting through the food and drink and household goods they'd picked up while the men lay sleeping in bed, still drunk and satisfied, and unknowing.

It was a fair arrangement, after all. The girls didn't ask to be taken on dates— no fancy restaurants, no lavish wooing was needed. Just a few drinks from a stranger in a bar and it was back to his place. He took what he wanted, and afterward, as he slept, Deirdre, or whichever of the roommates had got lucky that night, would hunt through drawers and cabinets and refrigerators, taking necessities while waiting for a cab to arrive. They never took money or items of value. Last November, just before Thanksgiving, one roommate brought home a twelve pound turkey.

The men, of course, were harmless. Not too good-looking, not too atrocious, and certainly never worth getting attached to. Tonight's guy, Deirdre figured, was married. His apartment was orderly, decorated with patterned, over-stuffed furniture, and when she'd inquired about the pair of gray high-heeled shoes tucked under the coffee table, he had replied "My roommate's. She's out of town."

Deirdre and the girls had laughed about this, too. "Typical," one said.

"Jerks," said another, sipping her wine.

Deirdre lit a cigarette, sat back in her chair, and pulled her legs up against her chest. She could still smell the man on her skin, and before she went to bed, she would take a shower. This man had been more attractive than most. His hair had been dark but thinning; he was dressed well in a leather jacket and slacks. There was something about him. Back at his place, he didn't compliment her as most men did; he didn't lie and tell her he loved her. He did not hesitate or stumble in bed, he stroked her shoulders, turned her over on her stomach, and when she said no, she didn't like it that way, he went on anyway, telling her not to worry, to relax. Afterward, as she searched his apartment for items to take home, it seemed too easy. The candlesticks lay in a box on the kitchen counter; the brie sat in plain sight on the top shelf of the refrigerator. It was as if these things had been set out for her, as if he knew this was all she was, a one night stand who would leave before he woke, who would take her payment of wine and candles and toothpaste and cheese and depart in a taxi, never to be seen again.

Deirdre unfolded her legs, leaned forward, and dropped the last of her cigarette into the empty wine bottle that stood on the coffee table. She picked up her purse from the floor. "I'm taking a shower," she said.

As she walked to the bathroom, her purse slung over her shoulder, she could feel something within it pressing into her side. The gray high-heels. She smiled, wondering how long it would take the roommate, the wife, or whoever it was who really owned them, to realize they were missing.

Kathleen Crow

Lessons

"Well, there's ten minutes of my life I'll never get back."

"Yeah, but you had it coming," my seventeen-year-old daughter Amy grinned impishly at me. "You really should learn to trust me."

"And just when did you get to be so manipulative."

"I learned at the feet of the master," she laughed.

"Sure, now you flatter me, you rat."

"I love you, mom," she said as she leaned forward and kissed my forehead. "So, you'll get Jeff to fix the ticket?"

"Yes, first thing tomorrow morning."

"You're the best," her voice trailed after her as she bounded up the stairs to her room.

"And don't you forget it either," I shouted after her.

Emotionally drained, I dropped my head to the kitchen table as soon as I heard her door close. Who would have guessed that a lifetime could be lived in ten minutes? One minute, I'm preparing dinner, happy with my place in the universe, and the next, I'm trying to find enough air to breathe.

The look on Amy's face as she entered the kitchen scared me half to death.

"What's wrong, baby?" I asked, afraid of the answer.

"I have bad news and devastating news. Which do you want first?"

Being the coward I am, I whispered, "Give me the bad news first."

"I got a speeding ticket. 36 in a 30 on Lamar, coming down the hill; you know, where the zones change."

"Oh baby, how could you?" I whispered. "Do you have any idea how much it's going to cost me to get my attorney to fix it so it doesn't show up on your insurance? Because Lord knows, if it shows up on your record, our rates are going to skyrocket."

"I know, mom," she said, blinking back the tears.

"So, what's the other news?" I asked, mentally trying to call up my attorney's telephone number.

"I'm pregnant."

Just like that, she blurts it out. I can honestly say I saw my life flash before my eyes and found that I wasn't quite as content in my world as I thought. "Oh my God," I wailed over and over again as I paced back and forth across the kitchen. "What have you done? Oh Lord, you've ruined your life. Have you thought about what you're going to do? You can't have a baby; you've got to go to college. But you can't have an abortion. What are we going to do?"

"Well, I think we should fix the ticket first and deal with the other stuff later," she supplied helpfully. I choked on my shocked laughter.

"What? You're worried about your ticket? You have changed the course of your life, and you're worried about a speeding ticket? Baby, forget the ticket. In a year, who will care about the damn ticket? We'll just deal with it and go on."

"Exactly," she grinned like an actress who had just won her first Oscar.

And then I realized I had been had.

Volume 1 Issue 4

As the curtain rose, the scenario began to play itself out.

David LaBounty

Exit, Stage Left

As the curtain rose, the scenario began to play itself out.

The battle at the beginning of act two had gone only slightly better than in rehearsals. The dragon fell to the stage before George could even raise his sword (sparing himself from the inevitable concussion). Now, George, his sword pointing in the air, smiled nervously.

"My job here is done," the voice whispered from his left.

George looked at his teacher, Mrs. Trumble, and smiled even wider. He turned back to the audience. Although he couldn't see them he knew they were out there.

George sheathed his sword and turned to the fair princess. "I tell you this," he said, "my love for you goes beyond what normal men may feel."

The fair princess's mouth dropped to the floor.

Mrs. Trumble frantically flipped through the pages of the script. "What is he doing?"

George placed his foot on the back of the dragon. A faint Umph! rose from the beast. "I did not slay this creature for the untold treasures promised by the King. I did not destroy this monster out of loyalty to the people of this town. Nay, my reasons were purely selfish." George turned back to the princess, his foot still firmly planted on the dragon. "I killed this dragon for the love of a woman." George held his hand out to the princess. "You, with the hair so red, the Sun burns with envy; you, with the brightest blue eyes that the oceans ripple with jealousy; you, with the sweetest voice, the robins weep with joy at the sound of it; you are the reason I laid waste to that awful beast."

Mrs. Trumble, after overcoming a momentary loss of voice due to shock, ran around yelling, "Curtain! Curtain!" in the lowest possible scream she could muster. But the rope was jammed, and the curtain would not lower.

George hurried over to the princess and dropped to one knee at her feet. "Can't you see the undying love I have for you that I would risk my life so? Is it not foolish to go on treating me like a child?"

The fair princess shook her head and then nodded and then just continued to stare dumbly at George.

George's shoulders slumped, and his eyes drifted to the stage floor. "I should have known that this would not have worked," he said in a small voice. "I cannot buy your love with something as trivial as this. I am not a man worthy of you—I am not a man."

Mrs. Trumble stopped her frantic movements back stage and listened.

George looked back at the fair princess. "I apologize for this vulgar display." He took her hand in his. "Some day I may be given the opportunity to truly express my love to you. For now, however, my job here is done." George lightly kissed the back of the fair princess's hand and stood slowly.

A few silent moments passed before the applause began. A roar of clapping and Bravos filled the tiny gymnasium-converted theatre. Even the fair princess was on her feet clapping. George looked off stage at Mrs. Trumble. Was she crying?

"George!" she hissed at him. "'My job here is done!'"

George snapped out of his daydream. He looked at the fair princess. She crossed her arms and stared angrily at him.

George turned back towards the audience. "Um…" he said, his voice shaking, "My j-job here is over—I mean done!"

There was a smattering of applause. George lowered his eyes and headed off stage.

Mrs. Trumble rubbed her temples. Three years of Shakespeare in the Park, five years on Broadway—including two Tony nominations, thank you very much—and now, here she was, Drama Director at PS 125, feeding lines to children who obviously had no passion for the stage.

God, she needed a drink.

Ed Phelts

A Tale Told by an Idiot

As the curtain rose, the scenario began to play itself out. Well, expect a pretty bizarre scenario when you let low-life into the Community Fine Arts Theatre. Like the unrelenting noise level of boorish patrons who, of course, go almost out of control at the sight of three big-bubbled, halter-topped, mini-skirted witches toiling over a cauldron of trouble. Or like the smell of fried chicken and red beans and rice surrounding the street person sitting next to you. Or his incessant, annoying chatter.

"Take the beans and rice, man!" He is insistent. And being rather intimidated by him and his seedy-looking companion who is cutting a huge breast with a plastic fork and a switchblade, I take the unopened container and a plastic spoon from his clean-enough hands just to shut him up. I hold it unopened on my knee, still trying to enjoy the unorthodox Shakespeare unfolding on the stage.

"Eat!" he insists again, while taking a bite out of a greasy chicken leg. I obey, opening the Styrofoam cup and eating a couple of spoonfuls. The man is happy. Smiling, he returns his attention to the stage and to his buddy sitting to his right. I silently curse the do-gooder who had the idea to open up the theater one day a month to street people in the first place. I silently curse myself for picking this night of nights to see the play. But it's my last chance to see this new production before it closes in a week.

As I close the lid on the cup, I am distracted by motion to my left, a few seats down. In the dim light, I can see a man with chin whiskers sitting with a thin, long-haired woman in a frayed, black skirt. He is stroking her leg. She uncrosses her legs. I return my attention to the stage.

Throughout the first act, the din from the audience remains rather constant. My chicken-chomping friends to my right appear to be napping. But there is an upsurge of chatter at the beginning of the second act as Fleance moonwalks on stage with his torch. I look again at the amorous couple seated a few seats away to my left. The fondling continues. Looking beyond the pair and in the row behind, I catch a glimpse of an apparently serious patron taping the performance. He holds one of those audio recording microphones in his lap. I do a double take. It's not a mike he's holding.

Macbeth is relatively short Shakespeare. It's a good thing, since I'm tiring of the audience, and my stomach is acting up. Nonetheless, I sit through the audience's cheering the murderers in the third act and whistling (again) at the witches in the fourth. Even though it's almost over, I decide to leave during the last act wherein Lady Macbeth exclaims, "Out, damned spot!" From somewhere behind me, somebody's dog, full of sound and fury, barks, obviously in refusal to obey the Lady's command. But I don't leave just yet. I don't leave until Macbeth begins rappin' his famous lament and somebody shouts that Broadway Annie sings it better. The thin, long-haired woman is starting to moan.

I strut and fret my way up the aisle toward the exit, leaving my cold rice and beans behind. I can feel it building. The exit door is oh, so far away. Suddenly, an unstoppable force "pulls my finger" with a vengeance. The resulting foghorn-like sound drowns out Macbeth, Seyton, the messenger, and even the thin woman's escalating sounds of passion. The foghorn persists.

The audience applauds.

Matt Miller
The Recital

As the curtain rose, the scenario began to play itself out. As if every move that she was making was scripted to tell a story, Margie Beth-Ann Armstrong, who now went by the name India, always dreamed of being a dancer. She strutted into the middle of the stage, dressed as a fireman, and removed the mock fire hose that she wore around her neck, instead of the traditional feathered boa. As she ran it between her legs, she gyrated in a circular motion. It was show biz, he thought, in its own way.

As he looked on from the back of the room, he couldn't help but feel proud. After all, it was his money that taught her how to tap and pirouette. He recorded all of her recitals, and it was his blood that was drawn while trying to sew wings onto a costume at the last minute because Tinker-Bell suddenly came down with the chicken pox. He had been there every moment of her life, and he supported her in every way that he knew how. So why should this be any different? It was still dance, he figured…only with less costume.

Donald Armstrong, at that moment, saw his little girl for the first time, under the same light that every other man in the world saw her. But in his eyes, it wasn't dirty or sexual. It wasn't without respect—like the way that he sometimes looked down his nose at the street walkers who hung out on the North avenue bridge on the weekends. It wasn't anything like that. What he saw was a beautiful woman.

Donald wasn't what anyone would call "a wild man." He wore beige and brown and sometimes black; he never wore bright colors. He didn't like drawing attention to himself. Hell, he never even took off his shirt on the beach. It was who he was, and who he had always been. He was the kid that swam in a t-shirt at summer camp. He slept in full length pajamas and socks. He even averted his eyes when bathing or changing clothes…so how could he have managed to raise a person that could be so opposite?

Margie was his life. Given to him on the day the only woman who had ever loved him (in every sense of the word) died. He had tried to raise her to be fearless, proud, and cool headed, like her mother—and he supposed she was. She was oddly cool when he told her he could only afford maybe two years of college at best. She said it was okay. That she had some money she'd been saving from working. He assumed it was from working at the Gap, where she had worked part-time for the past three years. And she was a smart girl—always had good grades. She could get a scholarship or a grant.

The girl stepped from the stage angelically, after disrobing the long coat that represented the rest of her costume, and she began to fish the men in the sea of tables for private dances at twenty bucks a pop. She made it to the rear of the club and had just hooked one, when she spotted her father.

"How'd you know?" she asked as she tried to cover herself.

"I was doing your laundry, and I found a check stub."

"I'm sorry, Daddy. Are you mad?"

"No," he said in the same kind voice that she had always known. "I've just never missed a recital."

Volume 2 Issue 1

The picture told the entire story.

Clifford Turner

Tavern Clown

The picture told the entire story. At least in my mind it did. I certainly remember the flash.

For the lack of anything better to do after the show that night, I was playing my bongos outside all alone on the balcony of a brewpub in downtown Mobile, Alabama. A half-hour earlier, I had said thank you and goodnight to thirty-five people from the stage of a struggling comedy club one block away. The drums sounded great, echoing down the narrow Bourbon Streetlike section of the humid, old city; but just as I relaxed and kicked it up into a fast funky rhythm, people from below, on the sidewalk across the street, began pointing and yelling up to me.

"Look, it's him!" one shouted. "It's the funny guy playing the bongos again!"

"Hey man, you were funny as hell!"

I remembered them, but typically, they could not recall my name. I had entertained them for fifty minutes as Ricky Mokel the "gifted idiot." A wise, but nervous and country talking, bongo playing nut who claims, "I think about stuff," and is always introduced as a last-second replacement for the headliner who is stuck in an airport. A good premise, and one that had supported a wife, two kids, and a dog and a cat for ten of the last seventeen years, yet the name refused to register. It carried sentimental value (my wife's first boyfriend's name) and seemed to fit the character, but Ricky Mokel was just not as memorable as Carrot Top, or Sinbad, or any other successful clown one can name off the top of one's head. The show was fresh, believable, and funny, but when recognized I was always, "That guy," or "The comedian."

Anyway, the moment I began to acknowledge my modest clutch of fans by answering them in my halting, high pitched Ricky voice, about to say something lame like, "I told y'all I was hyper!" there was a burst of light from behind me and to the right.

As if I was an aging and mellowed Sean Penn caught walking his pit bull by paparazzi, I instantly began negotiating for possession of the film. I believed the photo would be special: me in profile and in character, sitting all alone playing the bongos in a distant, semi-seedy local along with, possibly, the delighted upturned faces of five (count them!) fans. Something to frame and hang. The flash had illuminated what I predicted would be a nostalgic and telling moment about "The comedian."

For almost two decades, I had crisscrossed the country, calling home from Ramada Inns and worse. Being alone had become unhealthy. Of late, I had begun talking to myself as Ricky. I could not go on. Several times I had resolved to quit tavern clowning, but each time something—a new lap top computer, a nibble from television, or the sudden development of an entirely new act—would renew my energies and hope. Not this time, however. Time to go. Within a month, I would be selling Acuras in Atlanta. Perhaps I would use my Ricky voice at times to nudge a prospect to lease or buy.

I purchased the roll of Fuji film, after some creative begging, for the absurd amount of fifty-six bucks. Every dollar I had on me.

This might be amusing or it might be sadder than I realize, but the young lady who had visited the balcony and snapped the picture of me for no apparent reason had, unbeknownst to either of us, used up her twenty-four exposures prior to the final flash. I know this is true because I am at this moment sitting alone at my desk in the corner of a spiffy, deserted showroom sifting for a third time through two dozen snap shots of Alabama's finest street people, unable to find myself in this pantheon of goofs.

Richard Lee Zuras

A Photo of my Dad

The picture told the entire story. That's really how it ends, what I'm telling you now. But what happened before the photo someone had snapped of my father belting a man at our neighborhood bar—well, that's something to realize in itself. Understand that my father was no bigger than a fawn. Slight, thin-shouldered, thick-mustached. A fist like a child's.

But that night, deep into fall, my father walked me down to the corner bar, offered the door-guy a buck to watch me, and slipped inside. We had left my mother crying upstairs in our tiny fifth floor apartment. My father had forgotten his gloves, he had said along the way, rubbing Vaseline across the knuckles of his hands. He told me that the Vaseline would keep his joints warm. When I asked him if I could try it, he simply screwed the lid back on the container and pushed it back down into his coat pocket.

When my father came out of the bar, he handed the door-guy a buck, and I noticed a flash of red across George Washington's face. As we walked, my father took a kerchief from his coat and wrapped it around his hand. By the time we reached our building, the kerchief had stained red. Upstairs, my mom was sitting in the kitchen at the little yellow table where we always ate. She was smoking a cigarette, and big-band music drifted from the reel-to-reel in their bedroom. Glen Miller. My father's favorite. My father pulled out his wallet, thumbed the edge of the bills for a moment, and pressed a five-dollar bill into my hand. "Go to the movies," he said. "Get some popcorn." When I closed the door behind me, my father was holding my mother, and I could hear her crying and apologizing to him in a faint whisper.

When my father passed away, my mother sent me a shoe-box of old photos. "Remember him when he was young and happy," she said. And it was a strange thing, spreading these photos out across my bed. Baby pictures here, toddler age here, little-league, Pop Warner. One of him playing tennis with his father. Standing next to him, rising waist-high with grandfather's thick forearm crossing from his shoulder to his stomach. Dozens of photos of my father at his high school track meets—his hair black, slicked back, his shoulder blades cutting through his tank top. And always smiling. Grandfather once remarked that he could outrun anything.

And then the photo, black and white, of my father's fist coming off the cheek of a man I did not recognize. Behind my father, attached to the window, were the backward letters RAB S'ONEZ. ZENO'S BAR. And it came back to me. That day a man watched me for a dollar. That day my father didn't run from anything.

Chris Buchan

The Locket

The picture told the entire story.

Sixty-five feet, seven and one-half inches south of the point of impact, or measured laterally, thirty two feet, four inches from the curb, the shattered locket came to rest at the side of the road, just another mangled piece of wreckage among smashed and twisted pieces of glass and plastic and metal strewn across the pavement. It must have been separated from the breast of its owner by the force of the collision.

After sixteen years on the force, Dan had seen his share of accidents, but never anything as horrific as this one. It would take some rarified examination procedures to identify the remains. He had been fighting a continuous battle to keep down his gorge since the first instant he arrived on the scene. It helped to focus on the task at hand, meticulously sketching and recording all the trivial details: the length of the skid marks, locations of pieces of debris, and so on. It helped, a little.

The locket was hanging from the guardrail on the opposite side of the road, dangling, swinging like a pendulum in the gentle breeze, glimmering intermittently like a strobe beneath what should have been a full, romantic moon as it twirled round and round at the end of a fine chain. He reached out to take the little piece of gold in his hand. It would be okay to look closer; it had been photographed and recorded in his sketchbook already.

Amazingly, there wasn't even the slightest trace of blood on it, even though it had been partly crushed at some point. It occurred to him that strange things sometimes happen when violent forces interact.

The locket's cover was twisted into the open position, revealing a little photograph. Bemused, he turned his detective's eye upon it. It was an unposed photo of an attractive young couple in their early twenties, probably the occupants of the sedan. Smiling and happy they were, without a care in the world. Springtime, it must have been, judging by the apple tree they were sitting under; the tree was filled with little white blossoms. A happy young couple, out for a picnic on a beautiful spring day, sunny and warm, in the beginning of a beautiful little story about two young people, deeply in love, just setting out on their great journey together. He had a daughter about that age…

Snapping back to the present, and with an audible sigh, he put the locket into a little plastic bag. He'd seen it all before, but that didn't make any easier. Just a short while ago that locket was a private treasure, containing a snapshot of young hopes and dreams, a thing to be cherished next to the heart. But now it was just another piece of evidence, a record of all the might-have-beens that never would come to be, not after tonight. With another sigh, Dan shoved such thoughts aside and went back to work on his sketch, the locket deliberately forgotten.

Volume 2 Issue 2

The person on the train kept saying,
"I believe," over and over and over.

Joseph Horne

Train

The person on the train kept saying, "I believe," over and over and over. Her voice blended with the distant sounds of the oncoming trains and the inconsistent rhythm of the tracks rushing beneath us. Entering and exiting the tunnels did not change her vacant stare. The lights washed over her face. Her gaze went uninterrupted.

The car was nearly empty except for me and an elderly Asian couple. It was late, and Christmas Eve at that. Everyone else was at home where they should be. Only six more stops 'til I'm home too. Just six short stops.

I ride this train nearly everyday. Need directions on how to get CNN? I'm your man. Need to know how long it's going to take you to get from Perimeter to the Airport? I can tell you. Want to know how many blocks you'll have to walk from the Midtown station to Margaret Mitchell's house? Just ask me. I know these trains. I know their personalities. That's why I knew immediately that something was wrong. The train started slowing down as soon as we got out of Avondale Station. Something was up. She knew it too—only she knew better than me.

See, she knew about the other people on the train. The ones I couldn't see. The older couple looked concerned. Maybe they could see them too.

"When Hell open up, I'm gone see you in it."

The lady stood so quickly, we all jumped. Her voice booming at her demons.

"I say, when Hell open up, I'm gone see you in it. Yes, sir. I know you be there."

At first, I thought she was talking to me. This wouldn't be the first time someone expected to see me in Hell after all. As it turned out, she was talking to someone else. And it wasn't the Asians either.

The little couple picked up their bags and moved to the back of the train, looking out the window desperately for something. The lady started whispering to her husband, grabbing his coat.

"I believe, when Hell open up, your ass gone be in it. I'm gone laugh at you."

Her laugh erupted from some deep place inside that I suspect no one had ever seen. Her arms started waving, her entire body the opening act for a circus. Her large fleshy breasts were rolling and bouncing. The train rocked with her and started creeping along.

"I done told you. Hell gone open up and you be there. Yes! Yes! I see you there. And I gone dance and sing…"

And while Hell didn't seem quite ready to open up just yet, this lady was certainly ready for the dancing and singing part of it. And why not?

I made eye contact with the Asian lady. Her eyes thanked me for remaining calm and begged me to keep my position as a buffer between them and the dancing woman. The train had stopped moving again.

"Hell gone open up…and you be right there in it…in the flames…burning… dying…thirsty and hot…begging me to love you…but I ain't gone love you. Crazy? I ain't gone love you."

Having said her peace, the lady sat down and resumed her reciting of "I believe…" in a quiet monotone. The couple stayed in the back, the train started moving, and I looked into the frost my breath had left on the window.

At the next stop, the couple got off the train. I stayed with the lady though, hoping she might point out anyone else on the train that for some reason remained invisible to me. When my stop came, I picked up my backpack and slowly exited the train. She stayed on though. I think she looked at me when I stepped on the escalator. She rode on, grinning and chanting. I believe when hell opens up, she will see him in it. I figure he's getting what he deserves.

Lisa Firke

Winging It

The person on the train kept saying, "I believe," over and over and over. It reminded me of *Miracle on 34th Street*, that bit when young Natalie Wood almost despairs that Mr. Kringle can provide her heart's desire, but she's not ready to give up on it, or him.

It didn't seem likely that Santa had anything in his bag for the woman on the train. For one thing, she could have bought and sold Santa three times over: her shoes were genuine snake, and her sleek cat coat was the kind of faux that costs as much as real.

She closed her mouth when she caught me looking—which was all she noticed, just a man, looking. Others saw, however—saw, gaped, and, to my relief, doubted. I twitched my shoulders under my company overcoat. I was glad she had stopped saying, "I believe," or everyone on the train would have known.

The woman turned her face to the window, showing me a drawn profile and a heavy gold earring that resembled a wishbone. One hand fretted the front of the expensive coat and outlined the discreet swell of her stomach. She was pregnant, just beginning to show, and—I began to understand—terrified.

I would have to make a call on this one. My boss never keeps his cell phone charged, but with luck, I could reach his assistant. I punched the number, twitched my shoulders again, and turned away to ask, softly, "What have you got on the Greenwich Line?"

There was a sound of clicking keys; Assistant, checking her database. "There isn't much. Cardiac arrest; really angina. Some poor slob takes a tumble. Pickpocket cleans up during the confusion. And I've got a woman about to miscarry."

"Bingo." I said.

"Sad one. She's had three others. Getting a bit old for trying, if you ask me."

"Isn't there anything—" I let it hang. Assistant knew what I was asking; I knew the drill. I collapsed the phone into its case. A sequence unfolded behind my eyelids: the cramping would begin, "Please no," the woman would say, but the blood would seep through her faux fur and soak the sad plush of the seat. From the end of the car, the cardiac-arrest-that-was-really-angina cried out. This I could handle. "We've got to stop the train," I announced, pulling the cord. "Use the emergency phone," I told the woman, pointing on my way down the aisle. I was pleased when she rose and made the call without arguing—or marking the lone dot of blood that dropped by her shoe.

Having brought paramedics to the scene, I could have left it to them. A quick trip to the hospital, meds to stop the contractions, these might have been enough. But when the paramedics got on board, the woman got off.

"Wait," I said, but she didn't hear. I hurried after her, caught my heel in the rough stripping on the steps and fell sprawling to the platform.

"Are you all right?" She offered me a hand up. When we both had straightened, she withdrew and touched her stomach. "Ah. Oh," she said. "Oh, no."

"Expecting?" I asked. "My wife is, too," I invented. "The baby's just started to kick. May I?" She was too startled to say no when I placed a hand over her belly. Life feels good. I stepped back and smiled.

"A boy," I told her. "A good-sized boy."

Someone jostled me. I had forgotten about the pickpocket. He stopped at the end of the platform, flashed me a look, made a gesture at the collar of his coat that puzzled me, but I mirrored it anyway, the way you do when someone tries to signal that you have food on your face or your fly is down. I tucked a telltale feather out of sight. The boss gave me a thumbs-up, but slipped my billfold into his pocket and gave it a pat. Rules are rules, I guess.

I turned back to the woman. The grieved, haunted look had gone. "I believe you," she said.

Walter Addison March
On the Bubble

The person on the train kept saying, "I believe," over and over and over. A woman a few seats in front of him sneezed suddenly, and he looked up. In that instant of lost concentration, a couple seated to his right popped out of existence like a soap bubble at the end of its life.

Gerald Farnsworth went back to his chanting.

He tried not to think about the medicine coursing through his body. He desperately veered his mind away from the little chemicals swimming toward his brain. It was bad enough that they were on a mission to quiet his so-called paranoia, but to also disturb his all-important belief in reality as he saw it…that was down right dangerous.

Gerald glanced up. There were no other passengers on the train. He had been thinking about the medicine, and now he was alone…they'd all popped like soap bubbles.

"I do believe, I do," he sobbed and cradled his head in his hands.

The click-clack of metal on metal as the train ran along the rails reminded him of the click-clack of the pendulum toy in the psychiatrist's office and the noise it made when one ball swung in to pass its momentum through the other three and out the other side. Click-clack was a real sound, the sound reality made.

But behind him, when he was in the office, he could hear the doctor talking to Aunt Fae.

"This medication will quiet his mind and give him clarity. That clarity will cause him to realize that he doesn't need to believe in anything for the world to go right on existing." A small plastic case snapped open.

Aunt Fae sighed. "But won't it hurt him more to stop believing?"

"I think not. If I didn't think this was the best thing for him, I wouldn't suggest it."

A moment passed and then the doctor opened the office door. "Lou, could you help me in here?"

Gerald turned around to see the psychiatrist, with a syringe, and his burly nurse moving forward.

"No, you don't understand!!!" Gerald backed away from them. "I have to believe to keep reality going... if I stop thinking that..."

He started suddenly, realizing that he had lost concentration again—stopped believing again. He was no longer on the train. In all directions was a flat, featureless plain. It curved away, he thought, but wasn't sure because the surface was clear like glass.

He peered down. The surface swirled with colors, colors that danced and twisted at random.

As he looked at it, he realized that he didn't believe...not any more. Underneath him the colors bled away and the surface broke like a soap bubble.

Volume 2 Issue 3

My father and I left on a Thursday.

Greg Wahl

Under a Zorro Moon

My father and I left on a Thursday. To scorch some earth and never return. Although we shared—ever since kindergarten—the same time and place, we grew up differently. Sometimes it is hard to call him my father with our being the same age and all. But he is a priest, and better, my "father." Yeah, Father Gary Fitzhugh and Doctor Hector Acevado, two healers, one of the soul and one of the body, who lived their childhood under the El's rattle and grime in Chicago.

Only to find each other again decades later north of Ft. Wayne where Father Fitzhugh had a flock of souls and I had temporarily settled. As I tended to bodily repairs at a large hospital ER, Gary ministered to my spirit in that smiling style that I always admired and didn't know I needed.

As with anything chronic, the first hints were unremarkable. Certainly when he began to call me "He Tore," my little brother's pronunciation of my name when my brother was three and I was twelve, I suspected a possible problem. By the time Gary's homilies became uncharacteristic laughing fits of forgetfulness, it was now my father's time for help. With the Bishop, I arranged for Father Fitzhugh's immediate retirement.

So, off we went with no plans for the future other than Gary's happiness and every day new. Until the physician in me had to contend with the terminal stages, I wanted this selfless father to have a life of gusto.

First, we beelined to the Gulf to escape the snows. Gary splashed enthusiastically in the shoal and, while I was daydreaming, had his first sunburn since fourteen. I swore—I know, a sin—no more lapses. Sometimes in the brisk evenings, we went to beach bars thick with antics and, as usual, Gary saw just the fun. At one of those bars, I encouraged him to ask one of the women for a dance.

"Heck, with my luck she's a nun without her headdress," Gary chortled and shook his head.

We became continental drifters, and throughout it all, Gary maintained a faltering dignity, but a dignity nonetheless. Of course, he had his days, but for now, no pain. That made the slow decline less bitter.

Time the Terminator wore on. Making our way to the left coast via Montana in February probably wasn't the brightest idea, but Gary insisted on going "cowboy." Along the way, during a squall at a backcountry gas station, I waited for Gary to finish his constitution. Unable to feel, my weight caused the restroom door to crash open. There I saw Gary, with snow whirling about, trying to floss his teeth with his belt. That's a damn tough way for anyone. More alarmed, I noticed how his fly was unzipped for the umpteenth time. Man, I have to watch him better.

We approached the Oregon Pacific that spring. We were leaving the valley, heading towards a rack of barren hills, as Gary chattered about his adventures in Hudson Bay, a place he had never been but seemed to know well. The evening breeze swirled the clouds in front of a full moon as we made an upgrade. Gary sighed for a moment and then, with crinkled eyes that sparkled, whispered, "Zorro." And I could see it, too. A Sunday night, two boys on the living room floor in front of the black and white awaiting adventure.

Kristine Coblentz

The Goats of Heaven

My father and I left on a Thursday. We spent the whole next day in the city. I got to wait for him on big leather couches outside even bigger wooden doors. Out of the corner of my eye, I watched the lipsticked receptionists trying to type and pretend to talk to clients on the phone. I pretended to concentrate on my coloring book.

My father wrapped it up just in time for us to catch a taxi to the know-it-all-kids' science fair. All the way to the train station, we suffered through my brother's amazing feats of science stories. My father listened with one ear while his eyes strained to keep up with the driver's city street maneuvers. I hugged my bag and counted the hours until we would arrive at grandmother's.

Grandmother kept me busy all summer vacation, doing those things we missed not having a mother-figure around. We baked healthy heart muffins and made little pet animals out of things we found on our walks. Once she made a whole swing band of turtles out of rocks and shells glued together! We chewed mint from the garden for digestion and rolled our hair up in curls pinned tightly to our heads. Every morning, we took turns on the shake-your-fat-off machine. I was in heaven. My brother was bored by the end of that first week.

That's how he met the Baptists, got baptized, and learned to believe. He was just standing at grandmother's screen door one afternoon looking out, probably wishing he were somewhere else, when up to the curb pulled the purple bus. Jesus is Lord! it bragged in big white letters on the side.

Out of the bus door popped a wiry lady, a bible in one hand and a spray bottle in the other. As my brother told us later, she marched right up to him and asked straight out if he'd like to accept Jesus Christ as his personal savior. It must have seemed like the most exciting thing to come around the bend in a long time because he said yes without even thinking. Next thing he knew, the bible lady lifted her spray bottle and gave him a squirt through the screen door.

"Another one baptized in the name of our Lord!" she called out. She told him to watch out for the purple bus come Sunday.

After that fateful day, my know-it-all brother was never really the same. He is to this day, still the expert on anything and everything you'd ever want to know, and then some. But since he met the lady in the purple bus, specially-God-appointed-expert to the world has been his calling.

Science was left behind and prayer meetings became his favorite topic. At those weekly get-togethers, my brother and the Baptists would sing and sway and shout out while a skinny, red-faced man hollered at them and wiped sweat from his forehead with a dirty hanky. My brother relished retelling every fact and detail.

"And then three girls in the front fell down on their knees and saw the goats of heaven!" he told us, all excited.

"The gates of heaven...surely they saw the gates of heaven." My father furrowed his brow a bit.

"How would you know? You weren't even there!" my brother snapped back. He turned and stomped away, his Bible under his arm. I covered my mouth with one hand and tried not to laugh as I imagined him bleating for the Lord in the front row of that choir of great heavenly goats.

Tracie Clayton

Hold the Cards and Flowers

My father and I left on a Thursday. Our trip to New York wasn't a vacation, and mom wasn't joining us until Sunday. She was overwhelmed, making phone calls and writing notes.

Dad's college alumni newspaper had printed an erroneous obituary on him. When he called the associate editor to clarify, the guy said he didn't believe dad was still alive, had concrete proof that he had died, and wasn't going to stand for any prank calls. Dad then spoke to the senior editor, Casper Ewe, who said, "I don't know who you are, but quit teasing. Earl's dead," and threatened to contact the police if he ever called again. Meanwhile, mom got a lovely note from Fran Biedelmeyer, the wife of one of dad's classmates, and a tasteful floral arrangement from the Newmars. Len Price called and got my mom on the phone.

"Beth, I can't even begin to tell you how sorry—"

"Somebody goofed. Here's Earl." He and dad confirmed lunch plans for the following Thursday, the day dad decided to come to New York. Later that afternoon, Len called Casper Ewe and told him he knew for a fact that dad was alive because they'd just had lunch. Casper said, "Take it easy, Price. I know you and Earl were close. I can give you the name of an excellent therapist who specializes in treating delusions brought on by intense grief." Dad thought he'd better straighten them out in person.

Monday morning we went to Casper Ewe's office. We arrived just as he was running in with his *New York Times* and a leaky cup of coffee. Ewe was pale and speechless when he saw us. Dad broke the silence.

"Good morning, Casper."

"Earl? Beth? And this must be your daughter." The guy seemed even more shocked to see mom.

"That's right. Now do you believe I'm alive? Len Price didn't call that shrink of yours, by the way."

Casper spoke slowly. "But, Steve Nerke said you had expired. He sent us the death certificate too. And, Beth, I'm terribly sorry, but—"

"No problem. These things happen. I got some lovely cards and flowers."

"No, I mean the reason we didn't call you to verify Earl's death and express our condolences is that I overheard at a cocktail party that you'd passed away two years ago."

When I heard that, I thought it's a lucky thing mom's college didn't receive this misinformation and that dad's alumni publication doesn't print spouse obituaries.

Dad then asked the obvious question. "Well, why didn't I get a sympathy card then?"

"I don't know, Earl. I apologize, and I'll address this whole matter at the next staff meeting."

Dad thought for a moment. "Wait. Casper, did you say you heard about my death from Steve Nerke?"

"Yes."

"Then you're missing some other alumni news. Steve worked at the Medical Examiner's office for twenty years. He began making mistakes, was found to be insane, and was fired. A day later, his boss discovered that a stack of blank death certificates was missing. Plus, when we were in school a bunch of us got drunk one night and made a bet as to who was going to kick off first. Last year Murray Hemphil died, but Steve had bet on me. He was always a sore loser and couldn't take being wrong about anything."

Steve Nerke is due to receive a nasty letter from the alumni office, and Mr. Ewe promised to print a retraction of my dad's obit in the next issue.

Volume 2 Issue 4

I remember the radio was playing the best song.

Josh Beddingfield

I Fought 3 a.m. and Won: Kurt Weil vs. Outdoor Lighting

I remember the radio was playing the best song. "Snap, Crackle, Oompah, Fuck!" is how I remember it, but that wasn't its name. It was a kind of audio montage whose backbone was Kurt Weil singing pieces from the *Threepenny Opera* in German, accompanied by a wheezy pump organ. It was a very old recording; the scratch and pop of the aging vinyl sounded like a pinewood fire starting up. Rearranged samples of the Butthole Surfers would cut into the mix, guitars and voices barked like the shouts of a Tourette's sufferer.

"The old motorcycle will not get us to China! Fantastic Noodles! I'm a certified radiator now!"

It's the kind of thing that is brilliant beamed in at 3 a.m. from the community radio station 80 miles to the west. In the daylight hours, you just smile weakly at it and say, "That's weird."

Out of the window of my cabin, the stars were strung up bright as electric pearls over the gleaming snows of Mt. Adams. The dog eyed me from the corner by the wood stove; he was getting used to these late night antics of mine. The look on his face said, "I hope you don't plan on taking me outside at this hour."

"No," I replied to him, "It's too cold outside, and besides, I am naked."

It had started two weeks ago when a new neighbor hauled a dorky looking doublewide trailer onto the hill above my property. No sooner was the trailer operational then there appeared a brand new American flag on a pole and a great big mercury vapor light strung to the crotch of an oak tree.

Seriously bad neighbors.

I thought about shooting out the light the first time I awoke to see it shining in my bedroom window. However, there are limitations to these kinds of antics when you grow pot for a living. The thought of the Klickitat County Sheriff coming up the driveway to question me about the light was an ornerier proposition than lost sleep.

Of course, I considered asking them to take the thing down, but the more I thought about it, the more a dilemma arose in me. What if they said no? What if we got into an argument and they decided to keep a closer eye on me? Anonymity is my oxygen.

But it was getting toward the time when I would have to haul my seedlings across the hillside to the gully where they grow in the summer. I would have to make trip after trip in front of the spotlight carrying water, bat guano, peat buckets, and shovels. I couldn't tolerate having the light there either. It was them or me.

The song was reaching a wobbly crescendo of honking saxophones, groaning organs, and the word "Barbecue," repeated rapidly with an emphasis on a different syllable each time: BAR-Bee-Que, Bar-BEE-Que, Bar-Bee-QUE!

"What," I asked the dog, "would a Dadaist do about this?"

The dog sighed and said, "Cut off your hair."

Of course! The answer to the dilemma was to face its absurdity head on. I pulled out a pair of blue handled shears from the desk and went outside under the stars. Leaning forward, I gathered my long blonde hair into a firm knot on top of my head and hacked through it with the shears yelling, "That'll show them!"

The dog went back to sleep.

Kim Perrone

A Window to the Soul

I remember the radio was playing the best song. My fingers drummed out the bass line on the arm of the chair. I hadn't heard Def Leppard in ages, but they could pour some sugar on me anytime they felt like it. As I pushed the button to wheel the chair closer to the barely open window, my roommate began to snarl.

"Call in a complaint about that gardening man's ruckus, Lois. There are rules against radios on the grounds! I'm sure there are!"

As far as I was concerned, the music hadn't been loud enough. I only wish I'd had the strength to push the window open wider. I placed one hand against the glass. Its reflection would have reduced me to tears a few years ago, but I've grown accustomed to the gnarled knuckles and loose skin. Besides, I didn't have anymore tears left to cry over my aging shell.

"Put a cork in it, Jean," I spat. "If it's too loud, you're too old."

...Come on fire me up! Pour some sugar on me...

"I *am* too old! If you won't tell the nurse, I will."

The old biddy. She never would have complained to anyone but me. Stop that music, and she would have had nothing to gripe about. Unfortunately, the music did stop for her later that night. Medical reason cited? Old age. What did I think? Well, any vegetable is going to rot sometime. But that was it for me. Jean's death turned my life, whatever I had left of it, completely around. If I couldn't get my bones to run a race, I'd have to jumpstart the spark plugs in my head.

I began making demands the very next day. I made calls to my daughter, grandkids, whatever friends I had left. If I hadn't been feeling so sorry for myself during the last year, maybe the enthusiasm they showed for helping me wouldn't have come as such a surprise.

So, here I sit in my private room, my own radio playing whatever I want to listen to, and one heck of a kick-ass computer in the corner. Of course, if I could get around on my doddering legs, I probably never would have dreamed of owning such a passive device. Why play around in virtual reality when you can live life in the flesh. But that was the problem. I was a fertilized egg in a cracked shell. Plenty of potential on the inside, but that's where all the possibilities had to end.

Now my family calls me "CyberGran," but if they had any idea what I was doing, gazing into that monitor eight hours a day, they'd have me moved to a sanitarium. They'd never understand how I've entered a world where I'm worth more than the sum of my failing parts. For I have become Sam D.'s extra-marital cyber mistress, Susie from Ohio's junior high school confidant, single mom Karen's quilting buddy, stay-at-home-dad Michael's sports authority, and, oh yes, Stephanie K.'s personal advisor on the lesbian lifestyle. I bring new meaning to the phrase: "You can be anything you set your mind to."

Has dementia finally set in? Hardly. The truth is that I'm saner now than I have been in years. By day, I get to hop in and out of lifestyles I never experienced when I had my health. By night, I read up on the worlds of my alter egos. I'm even teaching my granddaughter to quilt now. Why yes, I am amazing. And I do believe I have a chat time opening of 2:00 p.m., Tuesdays, if you're searching cyberspace for someone understanding, passionate, and full of surprises. And the best part is, you don't have to hear Elvis blaring in the background.

Spencer Williams

The Lingering Death of My Electric Dream

I remember the radio was playing the best song. The best song I'd ever written, the only one that anyone dared to play on air. I burst into song over the worn speakers of thousands of South Texan's radios, edging in on the closing riffs of Led Zeppelin. No matter how often I hear myself on the radio, I can't help but smile. Not that I hear myself often. I think this radio station felt obligated to play my one song from time to time, since they had "discovered" me.

The dust billowed behind my car, filling the evening air with sand that filtered down to coat the leaves of the yaupon that grew wild along all country roads like this one.

Something else I've never been able to do is sing along with myself on the radio. Everyone else listens to a song and sings along and most of the time has their mind somewhere else. Me, I hear my song, and all I can think about is the day I recorded it. How my guitar just wouldn't go into tune. How the woman running the board smiled at me until she noticed my wedding band. How the doors didn't quite mute the sounds of another band in the hallway, practicing the songs they were about to record.

I kept the engine revving high, keeping the car running as fast as I could and maintain control. Still, I flirted with death on the turns, flying around them and calmly spinning the steering wheel as gravel threatened to carry me off into the trees. Somehow, I managed to keep the tires on the road.

The day the call came, that call that thousands of longhaired hopefuls wait for, I remember trying to wake up as quickly as possible. For any garage-band musician, the words "Arista Records" coming through a telephone are like an electric dream. I learned quickly that all of those stereotypical things you hear really do come out of the mouths of record companies. I was excited the first time they called me "Babe," just like in the movies. The last time I heard from them, it was "Mr.," and the message was, "don't call us about your next album, we'll call you."

The sun had probably dropped below the horizon. All I could see was the green trees that stood like parade-watchers and the tan gravel road. I drove aimlessly. *Parade's over a long time ago,* I told the trees.

The electric dream didn't last that long. Less than three years. I got the call, I recorded an album, I went on tour. The call was the best part. The album was not art, not even decent music, just a few extra tracks of padding to have a vehicle for the one song I wrote that made it. The tour was a blur of bars and rodeos and concert halls, all of which had one thing in common. They had people in them who ignored all of my other songs, and waited for the one, and as soon as it was over, they went back to their conversations or back to the bar.

I gunned the engine as I topped the hill. The car seemed to rise into the sky as if to take flight. It only lasted a moment. The car and I and the radio and the song all crashed back to Earth, the tires spitting gravel.

My wife, who had put up with me playing guitar until all hours of the night, had long since disappeared. That wedding band that stopped the cute board tech from flirting with me, had also disappeared, wrapped in tissue, into a small box in my dresser. And after the women stopped jumping up on stage to dance with me as I sang, after they stopped running their hands all over me while I tried to keep on, the house was as lonely as anything. My wife wasn't always the most fun, but she was always my friend. I missed that all the time I was on the road. A phone call was a pitiful substitute for her warmth, seeing her smile.

I had made enough money to keep us going for a long time, enough to buy the fast car that couldn't quite fly, enough to buy the guitars I'd always wanted, enough to buy the half-empty bottle that rode next to me, keeping papers from flying out of the passenger's seat as I abused the backcountry roads.

I picked up that bottle and uncapped it, taking a deep drink as I flew around another corner. A garbage truck prowled the other side of that corner, its driver's eyes quickly growing larger as I approached. I don't think I finished my drink, but I grabbed the wheel and threw it around as my heel stomped on the brake and clutch.

The car slid sideways and spun, but miraculously didn't flip over. The car and I and the bottle and the papers spun around helplessly until we took the bark off an old oak tree and came to rest at a wild angle in the deep drainage ditches that lay dry in the summer drought. The papers erupted from the passenger seat, almost seeming to take on a life of their own. Held together by a single staple, they rose slowly into the air and whisked away into the night.

My head thudding from the impact, I trapped the papers next to a stand of wildflowers. I caught a glimpse of my wife's signature on a solemn black line and an empty space hovering over another line right below it.

Volume 2 Issue 5

Whitney Heather Yates knew she was in trouble from the moment she learned how to spell her name.

E. Catherine Tobler

The Writing on the Wall

Whitney Heather Yates knew she was in trouble from the moment she learned how to spell her name. Girls weren't supposed to write to begin with, so spelling was unnecessary. Writing was left to the men and boys; they were the ones who went to school and worked to build a better world. Women made the world pretty, were responsible for babies. Writing and spelling were not needed.

The moment Whitney found the stub of purple pencil, she knew she had to try it. Her fingers curled around and she pressed it against the side of the house, the nearest flat surface. The pencil made a beautiful mark against the white paint; Whitney curled the W down and around, just as she'd seen on her brother's English manual. When she finished the letter, she stepped back and looked at it, grinning from ear to ear.

A glance behind told her no one was watching; it was midday and the men would still be at chapel. Momma was likely buried in the pantry, sorting the rotten turnips from the good ones. Whitney stepped up to the house and began to write the rest of her first name.

It had taken a long time to sort out the letters and the order they belonged in. With only brief looks at her brother's English manual, she hadn't had much time to sit down and work it out. Most of the work had been done while swinging from the branches of Old Haver's sycamore. For the longest time, she'd thought her name had a knee in it, but soon learned it was more of a neigh, like a horse might make.

She put a loop on the Y that ended her first name and brushed her fingers over the marking. The purple was pretty against the white paint; Whitney was certain it was an okay thing. Girls were supposed to make the world pretty after all, weren't they? But not by writing…or spelling…or doing much of anything that required thinking. And when Daddy saw the writing—

Whitney squeezed her eyes shut. Oh, she remembered well the day Daddy had come home to find Momma writing a letter. Just a letter, to her own

Momma in Gray Harbor. She didn't mean any harm by it, just wanted to let her know how things were. Of course, the envelope was addressed in a masculine hand. Someone was helping Momma and that just wasn't allowed. Daniel Averson disappeared a few days later; he was found strangled in some weeds in the creek a month later. Momma broke two fingers on her hand soon after Daniel went missing. Her fingers hadn't ever worked right since.

Whitney's name against the house was like a brand, newly pressed into tender flesh. The pencil had no eraser. There was no way to remove it. Whitney scrubbed her hand over the writing, but it only smeared a little. She told herself to calm down, to get in the house and see if there was an eraser in her brother's room. Surely there would be. There just had to—

A shadow fell across her name, and she didn't have to turn around to know Daddy was home early. She knew him by the outline of his hat. And she knew the shadow that followed, the snaking shadow of his belt as he removed it from his waist.

"First offense," Daddy said. "We go easy on that one."

The purple pencil sailed out of Whitney Heather Yates' hand, tumbling to lay unseen in the deep shadow by the gutter.

Mary Kay Lane

Saying Yates

Whitney Heather Yates knew she was in trouble from the moment she learned how to spell her name.

Before, when her mother called, "Whitney Heather Yates, you get in here or I'll beat your behind," she thought it might be Whitney Heatheryates. Or Whit Neeheath Eryates. But to discover, one awful day in kindergarten, that you were actually Whitney Heather Yates...now that was trouble.

In that small town, the name Yates was spoken in hushed tones by adults after the children were asleep. Sometimes older kids teased the younger ones. "I heard Bobby Yates coming with his chainsaw."

Whitney knew all the stories. She was as afraid of Bobby Yates as anyone. What she didn't know was Bobby Yates was her brother. What no one knew was that he escaped from prison and was coming home.

It had been a terrible day. Even though her kindergarten teacher insisted that no one cared her name was Yates, Whitney knew saying Yates was like cussing. She walked slowly out the school door. She didn't care how long it would take to get home. She had a lot of thinking to do.

Suddenly, a voice behind her called, "Hey, little girl."

Whitney turned. There was a man with hair so short his shiny scalp showed through. He was skinny, but strong looking, and had tattoos all over his arms.

"Where you going?" he asked.

"Home."

"Where d'you live?"

"I ain't supposed to talk to strangers."

"If we tell each other our names, we won't be strangers."

Whitney tilted her head. It made a little sense. "I'm Whitney," she said.

"Whitney what?"

Whitney stopped to consider. Here was a new person who didn't know that

Yateses were killers. Once he found out, he'd hate her like everyone else did. "Whitney Heather Gates," she said.

"Hey! Your name rhymes with mine." He stepped closer.

Whitney took a step backwards.

"Don't be afraid."

Whitney turned and ran, but with one quick move, he grabbed her arm and pulled her toward him. "I'm looking for someone. A girl your age. Her last name is Yates. Do you know her?"

Whitney shook her head fiercely.

"She's my sister. I just found out I had a sister. I want to see her. I ain't going to hurt nobody." His voice cracked a little so that Whitney almost felt sorry for him. He loosened his grip.

"You Bobby Yates?" She asked.

He nodded.

"How come you didn't know you got a sister? Everyone knows when they got brothers and sisters."

"Not when the brother does something bad, and the sister isn't even born yet."

Now everything began to make sense—why she and momma lived alone; why no one talked to them. "I think I might know your sister after all," she said. "Ashley Yates is in my class. I forgot since it's the first day."

"Did she say she had a brother?"

"No. We talked about families, and she just has a momma."

Bobby smiled. "That's good. She smart?"

Whitney nodded. "And pretty. Everyone likes her."

In the background, sirens wailed. Bobby sat down in the grass.

"They coming for you?"

Bobby nodded. Whitney Heather Yates sat next to him. "You ain't scared to go back?"

"Naw. Now that I know my sister's okay and she ain't ashamed."

Whitney reached out and patted his hand. "She's just fine."

Mari Whyte
"Why?"

Whitney Heather Yates knew she was in trouble from the moment she learned how to spell her name. With her insatiable curiosity as toddler, through early childhood, her favorite question was always "Why…?" Now, as early adulthood was fully on her, she knew she must discover the reason for her existence. This question had to be answered and answered soon, so that her life could continue. "Why am I here?" Whitney's question rang, again, through her mind.

Several times throughout her short life, Whitney either skirted or outright cheated death. She passed through treatment for a catastrophic childhood illness unscathed and in full remission, she experimented with drugs nearly to the point of insanity, and she placed herself in many unsavory and risky sexual situations without contracting any deadly diseases. He mother would call her "charmed" and would sigh, shake her head, and continue imparting wise, if not so welcomed, warnings. Her mother would say that she was being saved for something very special, but that she should not "push the envelope too hard." Whitney was compelled, however, to push, and push, and push. She finally chose a path that would allow her to use her energies to the fullest extent as well as provide her with the exhilaration of facing and challenging death on a daily basis.

"No, it is 300 joules for V-Fib," stated Yates with confidence. As with other highly disciplined organizations, the paramedics either used last names or an earned nickname. After two months on duty, Whitney was still "Yates." She was accepted and trusted by her male and female team members equally. Whitney had proved herself over and over in her short time on the job. No task was too challenging or too menial for Whitney to roll up her sleeves and tackle with equal drive and determination. On runs, she would assist with clarity of mind and quick assessment of need. She and Rowdy worked particularly well together. On an accident site, they would move, from the beginning, like one person. Whitney would hand Rowdy whatever it was he needed just as he turned his head to order it. It was whispered, none too quietly around the station, that Whitney was about to receive the rookie of the year award for the county. "This is what I was born to do," thought Whitney as she walked back to her bunk. "I have never felt more alive."

The alarm sounded the next run. Whitney made it to the truck and closed the door just seconds after Rowdy closed his. "Ready steady, Yates?" Rowdy chimed. "We're away, Pardner," answered Whitney as she lit off the siren and the truck sped to the freeway. The accident site was still a mess of confusion. They had made it there before the police, so the traffic was not yet under control. Grabbing one of the cases, Rowdy adeptly sped across and through the traffic to the mangled car in the median. Whitney was close on his heels with the defibrillator in hand. Seconds into their assessment, Rowdy ordered, "Hold the fort here, Yates, this one will need a back board." Whitney began her detailed assessment while opening her case to get vitals on the injured man. Glancing about to watch for Rowdy's return, she saw a tiny toddler climbing out of the car at the side of the road. No one on the road's edge could see her. The baby was heading, crying, across the freeway. The truck was coming. Whitney estimated, "Thirty miles per hour." Before she even knew she was moving, she had closed the distance between her and the baby, scooped her up, and pushed her up and into the air in the direction of Rowdy's outstretched arms. Just as she saw the baby touch Rowdy's fingers, a bright white light obliterated all else.

Vision, if you could call it that, seemed to be returning. Whitney seemed unable to focus; or perhaps it was what she was trying to focus upon that was the problem. He or she was the most substantial insubstantial person or being that she had ever seen. And what hospital had she been taken to? Scanning her environment, Whitney realized that, as the phrase goes, she was "not in Kansas anymore," but she was not even in any place earthly. Facing back to the being before her, she smiled in response to his (she had to call it him because it looked more like a he than a she).

He looked about to burst with something to say to her. Again, and for the last time in her existence, she asked, "Alright, I'll bite, friend. Why am I here?"

Moving his hand, he pointed behind her. She turned and looked at the accident scene being played out. She saw Rowdy still clutching the toddler.

The friend pointed to the baby. "That one," he said, "will discover the vaccine for childhood leukemias."

As peace washed through her and a smile grew on her face, she sighed deeply and replied, "Good answer."

Volume 2 Issue 6

It sounded like she said,
"Every day when I get home,
I find a naked body in the bed."

Hester Eastman
Just Making Conversation

It sounded like she said, "Every day when I get home, I find a naked body in the bed."

Gary stopped sorting through the mail. Elevator etiquette frowned on looking up when someone says something not meant for your ears, but when a person puts together the words, 'naked body in the bed,' in a public place, they're asking for eavesdroppers.

Gary recognized the speaker. Sara Brooks. She worked in IT. Her mail consisted of mostly computer magazines and fliers for programming classes.

Janice Harman, one of the Corporate Queens from the ninth floor was standing next to Sara. Her mailbox was filled with sales reports and important looking interoffice memos in large manila envelopes. In fact, Gary still had her mail in his cart. He could have given it to her right there, but Ms. Harman was too many floors up to touch her own mail. It would be sorted, read, and responded to by her secretary.

"Mm," Ms. Harman said, noncommittally. She was dressed in a light peach suit, hose, and peach pumps. Her bleach blonde hair tied up in a bun on back of her neck contrasted Sara's black and purple-streaked locks.

Sara wore black jeans, black boots, and a black polo shirt with the logo of the company above her left breast—standard wear for bottom dwellers. "It's not that I mind," she said. "I just wish she wouldn't bring them home every night. Why can't they bang away at his place once and a while?"

Ms. Harman glanced over her shoulder. Gary smiled and went back to sorting the mail. "How unfortunate," she said quietly, as if whispering in an elevator would give her any more privacy.

Sara leaned over to Ms. Harman. "I think they're interested in a threesome, you know?"

Gary, head bent over the mail cart, suppressed a chuckle.

"It's not that I'm a prude—I get my fair share of ass. It's just that my roommate is a skank. I love her like a sister and all, but she is a skank."

The elevator door opened at the seventh floor. Ms. Harman exited hastily as a silver-haired man in a blue suit got on. Mr. CEO. Richard Mercy. He had a separate cart for all of his mail. He nodded at Sara and Gary and pressed 11 on the panel. Then he turned and stared at the door.

Sara leaned over to him. "Every day when I get home, I find a naked body in the bed."

Mr. CEO glanced at her with a raised eyebrow before turning back around. She looked back at me and winked. "It's not that I mind…"

———————————

Sharon O'Hara

For Entertainment Purposes Only

It sounded like she said, "Every day when I get home, I find a naked body in the bed."

Madame Rene suppressed a frown, made a vague noncommittal hum, and went on staring at the luminous ball of glass while the client's peculiar statement hovered between them.

When the client did not continue, Charlotte Miles closed her eyes and drifted into her own reverie, leaving Madame Rene, her alter ego, deep in contemplation of the client's complaint. Or boast. Charlotte wasn't quite sure yet, and she was distracted by a different problem. The chair for the client still wasn't right. This new rattan bucket was far too low, and from the way the client had been fidgeting, must be uncomfortable, too. Hartford's would just have to exchange it, sale or no sale.

"I don't know what to do with them all," the woman's plaintive voice broke in.

Charlotte winced and reluctantly groped her way back. Naked bodies in her bed. Ugh. Now I'll have to listen to a stream of sexual fantasies. Still, she was determined to get through it all as gracefully as possible and give the client her money's worth.

"That is indeed a problem," she said, managing to sound both profound and coy.

"I know it doesn't happen to any of my friends," the irritating voice went on. The woman squirmed again, and this time there was a peculiar creaking sound. Damn chair! Spoiling the atmosphere.

Peering into the ball's expensively mysterious depths for a silent count of three, Charlotte suddenly flung her head back. She had practiced this to perfection in front of a mirror. Her cheeks were hollowed out, and fire seemed to dart from her eyes.

"You have called them from your hidden depths of magnetism," she intoned, fixing the woman with a hypnotic stare. "It is your time for fulfillment."

The client's face went a ghastly shade of grey. Good God! What on earth was wrong? Wasn't that what she wanted to hear?

"But they're dead!" blurted the woman. "I don't want anything to do with them. I just want it to stop happening."

A hot flush ran up Charlotte's throat and settled into two fiery spots on her cheeks. All traces of Madame Rene had vanished.

"I'm afraid I can't help you," Charlotte said at last in a flat voice. She didn't know where to look. There was an awkward pause during which she could hear the chair creaking and groaning like a tortured animal.

Charlotte forced herself to speak calmly but firmly. "Well. I think that's enough."

As the client departed, weeping now, and writhing, Charlotte was rigid with the effort to keep from touching her or being touched. But the door shut at last, and in a sort of daze, she began to prepare a pot of herbal tea. While the water boiled, she ate three large fudge cookies and put the rest on the tray to take with her into the bedroom.

Picking up the phone, she pressed the one unlabeled speed dial button. "Psychic Hotline," said a cheerful voice. Charlotte hastily verified her credit card and asked for Samantha.

"Oh, Samantha," she said, relief flooding her as she heard the familiar voice. "I've had the worst day!" She snuggled deeper into the pillows and reached for the cookies.

Joshua McDonald

The First Day

It sounded like she said, "Every day when I get home, I find a naked body in the bed." That's not really the thing I expected to hear on my first day at work and from my boss, no less. We work in one of those open loft spaces, so we're all out in the open, and I sit just 10 feet or so away from her.

Though, I have to say I was intrigued. She was a hot looking woman. As inappropriate as the thought was to have, I wouldn't mind being the naked one in her bed. You could tell she kept herself in great shape, and I could imagine how great she looked out of her clothes because she looked really good in them.

Now, you have to understand, besides just hearing her talk about this naked body to the VP of marketing, I also heard other key bits of this conversation. Things like: "took me," "hot," and my personal favorite, "pulsate." Yes, all this totally distracted me from the spreadsheet I was supposed to be putting together of the past three-year's expenditures.

What I was thinking about—way past the point I should be—was what it would be like to be in naked in her bed. I wondered if I would pass for "hot" in her eyes. Of course, I already had a girlfriend who was plenty hot, but my mind had kicked into overdrive about the possibilities.

"Jay?" Melissa tapped me on the shoulder, and I must have jumped 10 feet in the air because she was startled. "Jay, are you okay?"

"Oh…Yes. Sorry. What can I do for you?" She looked great today. Electric blue dress, cut so it was professional while accentuating her body just right. I hoped she didn't want me to go anywhere because if I had to stand, I'm sure we would've both been embarrassed by the physical evidence of my mind wandering way too far off course.

"How is the analysis coming?"

"Um…" I looked back at my computer screen, happy to see there were actually numbers on the chart. "I should be done…" I looked at my watch to see how much time I'd been in space—about 30 minutes. "It'll be about an hour or so. Definitely before lunch."

"Perfect. Listen, I'm going to work from home this afternoon. So when you're done, bring the printouts over to my apartment, and we'll go over them so you can make any changes we need before the presentation tomorrow."

My brain was spinning. Alone with her at home. There's no way I get to be the naked body. She'd never do that with her twenty-something assistant. But a boy could dream, right? "Great," I said. "I'll be over around three."

"Good. I'll tell my doorman to let you come on up."

As she walked away, my mind went back into overdrive. And, once again, I jumped when Danny came by to see if I wanted to grab lunch. I related the whole story to him.

"You don't really think she'd seduce you, do you?"

"Why not?"

"You're her assistant. She could be fired for that."

"Only if I told someone. Come on, Danny, she's hot."

"She's way hot, dude. So why would she even go for you when she could have anyone."

"Thanks a lot, man."

"That's not what I mean, and you know it."

"I don't know, it just sounded good, to be the naked body in her bed. I gotta finish this up. I'll catch you later."

I finally finished and headed over to her place. I kept trying to put everything out of my mind as I knocked on her door. "Just a sec, Jay," came her reply.

As she opened the door, I knew right then that tomorrow I would be the topic of the office gossip—and I was very okay with that.

Volume 3 Issue 1

"It was the only thing he couldn't do for her."

Miranda Garza

Through the Eyes of Revenge

"It was the only thing he couldn't do for her."

His wife's epitaph echoed in Marshall Hern's head while his mind's eye traveled back two weeks, to the last time he saw her.

The late afternoon sun had just started to show some color when Amy said, "Honey, if something ever happens to me…"

"What are you talking about?"

"I'm just saying, in case something ever happens to me, I don't want you to seek revenge. Promise me."

Before he could answer her, the grandfather clock chimed 5:30 p.m.

"Oh, Marshall, I've got to go."

"What's up?"

"I've got to meet with my informant."

"Who?"

"You know I can't tell you that." She reached over to give him a kiss.

"P.I.'s are so secretive," he complained.

"Ex-assassins are so nosy."

"The term is equalizer. Assassin sounds so barbaric."

The last picture he had of her was when she turned from the door to wrinkle her nose at him. Four hours later, she was discovered in the Brazos River with the car wrapped around her. The police said she lost control of the vehicle.

Though the news hit him like a bullet to the chest, he forced himself to think about her 'accident.' It hadn't been coincidence that Amy brought up the subject of something happening to her.

Marshall headed for her file cabinet. Knowing her system, he quickly located the folder labeled Current. According to her notes, she had been hired to look into the murder of a reporter who had been investigating some missing city funds before his death. Amy worked on the case for three months, and with the help of her informant, Trippin' Eddy, found out who killed the reporter. She'd been about to break the case wide open.

Marshall dialed a number.

"Hello."

"I need you." Hanging up, he flipped through the photos in the file. The mayor proved to be the common factor in all the pictures. Transcripts of taped meetings with his accountant showed concerns about diverted funds and a private bank account. Marshall's heart ached over the phrase 'she knows too much.'

At 10 p.m., Marshall walked down Main Street to Mocha's Coffee Shop. Soon after he sat down, a small woman entered through the back door.

A few years ago he'd been paid to terminate her, an FBI agent/informant. He remembered her courage as she starred down the bore of his silenced Walther. It seemed a shame to deprive the world of such courage and nobility, which is why he helped her escape instead. She chose the same city Marshall did to disappear; only now she's a police officer, and he decided to retire.

"I'm sorry about Amy." Moriah Nolan took the seat opposite him.

Marshall only nodded. "I want the police report on her accident."

She handed him a folded paper from her pocket. "When you called, I made a copy."

Marshall read the report. "1.8 alcohol level?!" He drew both hands to his face. "She wouldn't even buy rubbing alcohol."

"Murder, then?"

His face hardened, and he pushed Amy's case folder across the table. "Here's the proof. Make sure it gets into the right hands."

Without hesitation, Moriah nodded and opened the file. If what she saw surprised her, it didn't reach her face. She rose.

"He's having lunch with his accountant at Oasis at 2:00 tomorrow." Without another word, she left the shop the same way she came.

Marshall stationed himself on the roof of the building across from Oasis at 2:30. He watched the mayor and accountant rise from their table and pay the bill. The mayor laughed as he came out the door picking his teeth. Marshall heard his wife's voice. 'Promise me, you won't take revenge.' The scope's cross-hairs rested on the man's head before the silent shot.

It was the only thing he couldn't do for her.

Nick Aires

The Bonda Prophecy

"It was the only thing he couldn't do for her."

Vera looked at the Royal Paige and smiled cruelly. *At last!* she thought. *There's something that that charlatan sorcerer can't pretend to conjure up for the Queen!* Vera's chance to upstage her nemesis had come at last. But she was torn; she didn't want to leave her apprentices alone.

Earlier that day, the sorceress Vera had been gazing into her crystal ball when she'd received a mildly upsetting vision. She'd seen her apprentices, Hiro and Cassie, feasting on her prized *bonda* fruits. All week, she'd been snacking on the rare fruits in front of them while they practiced their spells, but she'd never shared her treats with them, much like she didn't share *anything* with *anyone*.

Just before the Royal Paige had arrived, Vera had been munching on some of the sweet bondas. She didn't want to dally and keep the Queen waiting, but she was concerned about leaving the children alone with her delicacies.

This is just too important to pass up, she thought.

Since her apprentices did not even recognize the fruit she'd been snacking on, Vera fallaciously told them that a man who hated children grew bondas in a magical orchard. She warned them that there was a spell on the fruit that caused rocks to fall on the heads of any children who ate them. Certain that she had sufficiently frightened her apprentices, and having ordered them not to leave the house, Vera went off to the palace.

After Vera was long gone, the magicians-in-training looked at each other, thinking: *Should we?*

After many excruciatingly indecisive minutes, the curious children approached the bowl of bondas. "We'll just look at them," they giggled. "Surely it wouldn't hurt to *smell* them," they agreed.

The bondas smelled delicious, with hints of strawberry, coconut, and kiwi. The children couldn't resist temptation—they greedily gobbled up several bondas.

With full stomachs, the apprentices were aghast by what they'd done, belatedly remembering Vera's dire warning. They dove to the floor, and placed their hands over their heads.

"Hey!" said Hiro after a while. "I don't think the rock shower's coming! She tricked us!"

"Yeah!" Cassie exclaimed. "But she's still going to have our hides when she gets back!"

"Hmm, maybe not..." Hiro picked up Vera's crystal ball and smashed it on the ground.

"*Are you crazy?!*" Cassie shrieked. "For the fruit, she maybe would have made us conjure stinkweeds or something, but for *this*...I don't even want to think about it!"

"Relax! I have an idea—just get back on the floor, and pretend that you're expecting rocks to fall on your head."

Soon, the sorceress returned. Entering her study, she stopped short, staring at the shattered remains of her crystal ball. Enraged, Vera shouted: "What do you have to say for yourselves? And why are you cowering on the floor?"

Hiro stood up nervously, still covering his head, and said: "Great Sorceress, while playing tag, we accidentally bumped the crystal ball."

"We are *sooo* sorry!" Cassie chimed in.

"Because we were awfully upset by the accident," Hiro continued, "we sought punishment for our inexcusable recklessness. So, we ate some of the cursed bondas and were lying in wait of the rocks that we were sure would befall us..." Hiro looked up at Vera coyly. "But perhaps the rocks were unable to penetrate your roof...?"

If Vera had only shared, she would still have some of her bonda fruits left, as well as her crystal ball. The sorceress learned an important lesson that day: Don't take on any apprentices.

Ben Lareau

Only Things

"It was the only thing he couldn't do for her."

"Why?" I knew he would ask this, as surely as I knew it had been a mistake to even begin discussing this.

"I'm not really sure. It's just what he said to me before he left."

And of course, he had to ask: "So what is she up to now?"

"I don't know…I've tried to get a hold of her, to get her out of the house, but either she's not there, or she's just not answering. I think it's going to be a while before she feels like doing much of anything." Please God, I thought, let that deter him from making an ass of himself for at least a week.

He said nothing for a while. The porch was dark—the light had burnt out two nights ago—but I didn't need to see him to know what he was thinking. Much of the time, people's predictability, their own personal trademarks, make them likeable. Other times, they make them despicable, like a dog that refuses to stop mounting your leg.

James had sighted a leg, and his haunches were already aquiver. He'd already tried with her; though not in the conventional sense of one concrete action—it was actually a painfully slow, long, awkward series of advances, retreats, parries, and still more advances.

"How long did Lynne know he was leaving?"

"As long as it took him to move his stuff out."

"Jesus. What an asshole," he muttered, bathing in now-righteous fury towards his old opponent—who happened to be a friend of mine and once a friend of James as well.

"Well, I'd best be leaving," he said, after a minute of making the appropriate stirring noises. In the dark of the porch, I could sense him looking at me, trying to gauge whether or not I'd picked up on what he was thinking of doing. I was glad I hadn't replaced the light.

"Have a good one. Give me a call next week about that Bumbershoot thing."

"Yeah, will do…"

I sat on the porch, watching his tail lights cruise down the street in the direction of his own house. But I knew he'd double back in a few blocks and head down to her house. If she was lucky, she'd still be too depressed to answer the door.

Steve had told me before he left that the one thing he couldn't do for her was to stay. The one thing James could not do for her was leave. Was this really what things boiled down to between people? The inability to do something else? I thought about my own relations, trying to fit their pegs into this new-shaped hole: my inability to tell James to leave Lynne alone, for example. Or the fact that Mary would be home soon, probably drunk—all of it really boiling down to my inability to abandon the parts of myself owned by other people: the parts now dying like their owners.

After a minute of this, I stood up and went to the phone to dial up Lynne and warn her not to answer her door.

Volume 3 Issue 2

The party was only the beginning of what would happen tonight.

Kelli A. Wilkins

Guest of Honor

The party was only the beginning of what would happen tonight. Devlin smirked and surveyed the parlor. Longhaired young people lounged everywhere. Couples talked and laughed in the corner near the gold and green paisley draperies. Others were sprawled out on the orange carpet, drinking beer and smoking a pungent herb. Music blared from a wooden stereo cabinet. Black candles burned in cast iron candelabras. The scent of musky, earthy incense filled the room.

This soiree began Gregory's so-called ritual. He said it liberated the mind, but it was nothing more than a diversion to get everyone drunk and high. The occult craze was in full force. People were trying to summon Satan for petty things: fame, fortune, and women. Nothing important like conquering the globe or changing history, something that would be interesting for a change. Humans had become boring and unimaginative.

Devlin arched a pointed eyebrow and sipped a glass of Merlot as he watched Gregory, a tall man with stringy blond hair, circulate among his "followers." The group hadn't noticed Devlin, or if they had, assumed he belonged there. He ignored them. It was Gregory, the leader of this pathetic little coven he'd come for. After all, he'd been invited, summoned even. It would be in poor taste not to appear. Gregory had rehearsed his script for this evening, reading from the book, dramatizing the incantations over and over all afternoon until Devlin could stand it no longer.

His eyes focused on the ancient book Gregory held in his hands. It was a large, leather-bound volume. He knew the contents well. It once belonged to him. At some point in time the invocations had been translated into English. Sadly, Devlin realized that they had lost most of their charms in the conversion.

Gregory clapped his hands. "Let's start! It's almost midnight."

They formed a circle. All lights except for the black candles were extinguished, the racket from the stereo silenced. Devlin stood just outside the group to watch the performance.

Gregory opened the antique text to a marked page. He closed his eyes and tilted back his head. "By the power of the Black Arts, we summon ye, Demon of the Night, Master of Chaos! We beseech thee to do our bidding!"

There was no sound for two full minutes. And then, as practiced...

Gregory held out his hands. "I sense it! He's here! The Lord of Darkness is here!"

Devlin gazed around at the audience. Most of them looked bored with the charlatan. He smirked. A rumble of thunder boomed outside. The candles flickered and winked out, immersing the chamber in darkness. Devlin's cat-like pupils permitted him to see what mortals couldn't. Gregory's eyes were closed, the book clutched to his chest. The door and windows flew open. People shrieked. An icy, rank breeze filled the room. At his silent command, the drunken cult members screamed and bolted for the door. They shoved and jostled their leader as they pushed past, nearly trampling him and each other in their haste to escape. Devlin steadied Gregory with one clawed hand, ensuring that his book was safe.

"Wait! Where are you going? This is what you wanted! Don't you see?"

Within seconds the room was empty, the cultists gone. Gregory fumbled to a lamp and switched it on. Devlin appeared in his natural form. He grinned as Gregory gasped and stepped backward.

"Who are you? What are you doing here?"

Devlin moved toward the trembling man and chuckled. "I was invited."

Ehren Hemet Pflugfelder
The Distance Between People

The party was only the beginning of what would happen tonight. There was a time, after a party and a day within a year that started with a nineteen and ended in a number which isn't really important, but it was seemingly terrifying in the height that two digit numbers go. And this year existed, for the time being (the time being in an hour with the moniker "PM," though the exact hour was not known either to the people in the story nor the outside observer), and being in the time were two people, a boy and a girl that could also be represented by a young man or woman. The young man had a name that was my name. The other person in the equation was his girlfriend, a lovely young woman who was where she was, and where she was was a college where she could major in creative writing with a certain trend towards feminist literature and postmodern theory of the quirky sort. As it happened, this person who was going out with a creative writing major from Pitt, decided that he wanted a Sheetz brand "cup o' chino," a drink that is essentially a poor man's cappuccino, explaining why the young man in the story drank so many; the specific flavor of "cup o' chino" he wanted was vanilla. He wished for a vanilla "cup o' chino." They were out of vanilla. He was understandably upset and greatly distressed, though the distress he possessed was an inward sort of distress not particularly obvious to the other customers at the Sheetz, or his girlfriend, the creative writing major. She suggested that he should get the next flavor over on the machine, which was diet vanilla. While repulsed by the concept of anything emblazoned with the title "diet," he filled a 16 oz. cup with whatever "chino" substance was in the machine and went to pay for his drink and a packet of Reese's Pieces with valid U.S. currency. The Reese's Pieces would be excellent to eat if the young man decided to get high that night with the creative writing major from Pitt, they weren't sure if they would or not. While putting the lid on his low calorie, froth covered, and caffeinated beverage, he noticed a spider, probably dead, presumably dead, floating on the diet vanilla flavored foam; the premature death of the arachnid most likely due to something diet in the "chino" and not the scalding temperature. While mildly repulsed, he showed the spider infested foam to the cashier and she said in her nicest voice that he could get another one free of charge. He surmised that the entire batch of "chino" was probably tainted, so he declined and instead purchased an ice tea beverage that was sealed for his own protection. On the way home, he drove over a speed bump he never noticed before, merely jostling the ice tea beverage that sat between his thighs (as a note, all of his cup holders were broken in the great Slushee accident of '98). It is of note, however, because if he would have been holding the diet vanilla "cup o' chino" between his thighs, and had hit the same bump, and hadn't put the lid on correctly, he might have spilled the beverage and suffered permanent testicular burns, scarring him for life and impairing his future ability to father miniature versions of both himself and the creative writing major whom he was visiting for the weekend.

John Tennel
Picture Imperfect

The party was only the beginning of what would happen tonight. I know this because I can see into the future. No, I can't tell who will win the Super Bowl or which stock is going to be the next IBM. If I had those kind of powers, I wouldn't be wasting my time here with you.

I'm also not speaking metaphorically. I see moments in the future. Polaroids of time—underdeveloped images that can't be tied together in any coherent pattern. Like déjà vu, only it's not.

I was at the gym, playing racquetball, when an image formed on the white wall. It was dark. A crumpled car sat in the middle of a tunnel. Didn't look like any vehicles my friends or I owned. Nevertheless, I stayed away from the midtown tunnel for two weeks. I added a half an hour to my commute each way, but I wasn't going to take any chances.

Then, one night, Brokaw or Jennings or Rather broke in with the news of Di's accident. Those poignant pictures from Paris were first shown in my mind two weeks earlier.

But you don't have to believe me—probably won't in fact. Because I am telling you this story after it happened, you may just assume I made up the whole soothsayer bit as an excuse. I really don't care.

It didn't even start out as a party. It was just going to be a few friends getting together, tossing back a few Buds, watching the game.

But I knew better. In the shower this morning, I saw a flash of people—strangers—frozen in mingle-mode around a large silver barrel. And a dog. Another one of my Polaroids.

That one was easy to decipher. The naked woman I saw in the mirror while I was shaving was a little more coded.

She was on her side, her bright white skin standing in stark contrast to the blue sheets of an unfamiliar bed.

I cut myself.

The scene faded in the bathroom steam. That's the problem with most of my premonitions—they're about 975 words short of a thousand.

John called me at work.

"We're getting together tonight."

"Who's we?"

"Me, Sam, and Mike. Thinking about grabbing some Buds and watching the game. You in?"

I should have said no. I should have made some lame excuse about Jenny wanting to go to the movies or dinner or wanting sex.

"Yeah, I'm in."

I showed up at John's place a little before kick-off or tip-off or face-off. Jenny was pissed, but her mother called complaining about her sciatica or her shrinking uterus or whatever she complained about that sent Jenny into fits of compassion that had her flying to her mother's side where she would stay until she talked her out of her depression.

"Where are the guys?"

"Beer run."

What happened between my sitting on the couch and our arrival at the party is irrelevant. All you need to know is that the game was over before the first quarter, so Sam suggested we crash a party thrown by some guy at his work.

You know what I saw when we arrived: a keg, strangers, and a dog.

I mingled, met Cindy, and fell in love. Not some puppy dog lust, but soul-aching love. I knew right away she was the naked woman in my mirror.

Cindy and I talked, we exchanged numbers, and I promised I'd call.

When Jenny got home, I told her it was over. She screamed, threw dishes, set fire to the couch. I wasn't too upset. I saw the entire scene a few days ago on my computer screen at work.

That's the problem with seeing into the future, even if it's just snippets. There are very few surprises. For me, though, there's no order to the images—I never know which future will come first.

At least it keeps me on my toes.

Volume 3 Issue 3

Hal couldn't sleep.

Chris Salter

The Box

Hal couldn't sleep.

This wasn't entirely surprising, as angels don't naturally sleep anyway—they are, after all, eternally vigilant, and sleep precludes vigilance—but Hal was frustrated anyway. Michael himself had given him the task of deciphering why mortals did the things they did, and Hal had promised the results within a century.

That had been nearly four thousand years earlier.

Hal had studied and studied and studied, and watched from on high, and then descended and taken a mortal body for a time to join in the experience, but he couldn't seem to understand what drove the mortals. Michael followed Hal's research and sent him encouraging messages, saying he understood that the problem seemed to be larger than anticipated, but Hal couldn't help but grow desperate. Finally, he reached the decision that sleep was the answer. He tried everything else that humans did, from eating and drinking and even expelling waste—all the way to fornication, once he gained the requisite permissions. Hal's insights into human nature led to major reforms in Heaven's dealings with mortals, but still, Hal couldn't quite get a grasp on the way their minds worked.

Take religion, he told Michael one day when his work was being reviewed. God himself takes mortal form, even gives the mortals proof of who he is, orders his followers to be nice to people, and they decide to kill everyone around them. It makes no sense! he cried, and Michael had nodded sagely and left him to his work.

In the end, Hal experienced everything a mortal would ever do in its life. Everything but sleep. So he came to the conclusion that he must learn to sleep if he wanted to understand the mortals.

He tried lying in a comfortable bed for several years, and nothing happened except that he stared at a lot of clouds. He tried imbibing spirits, and even drugs (with appropriate permissions, of course), to make him sleepy, but being an angel, he was immune. He even resorted to counting sheep, as one helpful mortal had suggested, but he finished counting the world's sheep long before he felt tired.

Finally, Hal decided that the only way he would ever fall asleep was to find a way to bore himself so greatly that even angelic vigilance faltered. So he began searching for the least interesting activity that one could engage in.

Hal searched for years, roaming the Earth disguised as a mortal, trying his hand at every profession. Years passed, but each job was as interesting as the last, giving him ever more insights into the mortal mind. Years stretched into decades, and then into centuries, and around Hal the world changed. Huts gave way to large houses, and in turn to skyscrapers. Horses gave way to cars. The change that interested Hal the most, however, was when word-of-mouth was replaced by radio, which in turn was giving way to television.

Television! Hal was astounded by television. With such extraordinary promise for the advancement of their species, the mortals turned instead to "sit-coms" and "reality shows." Finally, Hal bought a television set. Miraculously, he found himself bored! Still, there was a certain appeal to it all, and he was just interested enough to be kept awake.

And then, one day, Hal slept. His apartment, which he rented so as to fit in among mortals, was dark. In front of him, the television flickered and flashed, and a badly-dressed mortal was saying, "And the award for Best Actor goes to…"

Joy L. McDowell

Cutting Losses

Hal couldn't sleep. He kept hearing tires screech as the whiteface went down in Sacramento Boulevard traffic. Money down the gutter. Time wasted. He clenched his jaw and dragged his fist along his forehead, but the image of fat, little Carl chasing the calf's trailing rope halter across four lanes elbowed him further from sleep. Having an animal breathe its last, not in the fairgrounds livestock barn, but a block away on urban asphalt was a cattleman's nightmare.

California wasn't Texas. There might be a lawsuit. The young gal in the BMW had made a lot of noise about her mucked-up car. She should have been thanking her lucky stars that calf didn't come off the ground and send a rump roast right through the windshield.

Hal wrestled over onto his left side and let the bed sheet drift off his shoulder. A flowery scent wafted off Lorraine's hair where she nestled against her pillow. His thoughts circled around the accident scene, then the uglier, family scene, a regular box canyon he had herded himself into. Lorraine was a sweet package. She worked steady at her nursing job in town and pitched in at the ranch, always rustling up dinner if her shift put her in their kitchen on time, but her fat-assed kid had their life going to seed in a heartbeat. The 4-H calf project had been Hal's last attempt to get something going with her boy.

Carl didn't have much to recommend him—a flabby body, one bad attitude, and about as much energy as a hog flopped behind a corn trough. Hal's calloused hand brushed against his wife's sloping hip. Even a good heifer could throw a bad calf with help from a second-rate bull.

The air conditioner hummed in the window. August heat choked the night. Down the hall, Carl slept in the bedroom that used to belong to Darby and Reba. His girls had raised goats, sheep, calves, and a llama for fair projects. They had managed their animals without causing a scene or costing the ranch any loss-column money. But simple chores, like shoveling manure or tending his own stock, sent Lorraine's kid into a bellyaching yammer. All he was good for was eating junk food in front of the TV and fattening the long distance phone bill. More than once, Hal heard him whining to his father about how hard he was forced to work on the ranch.

If a man could go to hell for hating a twelve-year-old, then Hal was doomed. That bloody calf bellowing on the oily pavement had cinched it. At least the cop let him fetch his snake pistol from the truck and take care of the suffering animal.

Hal scowled at the fan bolted to the bedroom ceiling. The whirring blades stirred his thoughts like a disk plow busting into hardpan clods. In the morning he'd talk to Lorraine. Either Carl went to live with his father or the marriage was over. The ranch was Hal's life. Having a woman in his bed, well, that had always been an extra.

Michael Kelly

Learning to Fly

Hal couldn't sleep. He woke early, rose, went to his bedroom window, lifted the sash, and breathed deeply.

Hal smiled.

A warm wind blew gently, stirring fallen leaves, moving across trimmed lush lawns and neatly swept walks, whispering secrets that no one heard. Downstairs Ruth-Ann Maguire sat at her kitchen table sipping coffee, enjoying the calming current from the open window, waiting for her lacquered nails to dry. Birdsong trilled sweetly in the thin mountain air, and she smiled. Placing the ceramic mug down, she went to the window and peered out. High in the maple was a nest. Funny, she hadn't noticed it before.

Busy, she thought. Always busy. No time to sit, relax, enjoy the little things life had to offer. Too busy with work, work, work. Christ, she needed a vacation. Earl, as well, she thought. And Hal, her son. She hardly remembered what he looked like. Ruth-Ann shook her hands, blew on the cinnamon-colored nails. Movement caught her eye, and she noticed a small bird fly into the nest, a fat red wriggler trailing from its beak.

As a child, she remembered now, a wee baby bird hopped about in her back yard. She'd grabbed her mother and ran to the yard to scoop up the pathetic creature. But mother had prevented her, saying birds often fell from their perch, that they'd make their own way back to the nest when their wings strengthened. Besides, admonished mother, you wouldn't want to get your scent on them, they would never be welcomed back to the fold.

Later, heart sinking, and the tiny bird flapping useless wings, Ruth-Ann watched helplessly as a big old tomcat came by and gorged itself on the defenseless hatchling.

Ruth-Ann wondered what it would feel like to have her child leave the nest, to be powerless to help him. Wondered if Hal had developed his wings yet. The thoughts scared her. Poor child, on his own.

Yes, she'd have to schedule some time for Hal, get to know him again, test his wings.

A horn shrilled loudly. Ruth-Ann watched the minivan pull up to the boulevard. Her ride was here. She grabbed her briefcase and bolted out the door, sprinting down the driveway to the idling van.

The wind picked up, blowing chilly pockets of air along the wakening street. Dark clouds rolled along the far horizon.

Upstairs in the quiet house, Hal noticed the bird's nest resting on a branch in the tree directly opposite his window. A bird, feeding her young, eyed him warily with flat black eyes.

Hal went to his bed, fished under the mattress until he found what he needed. He went back to the window and leaned on the sill.

He grinned. Things would be different today. It was time to leave the nest. He would show them what an odd bird he was.

So what if he refused to wear their clothes, listen to their music, and join their cliques. He was used to their suspicious stares, their whispered secrets.

Hal studied the bird and her young. The mother stared back at him, protecting and nurturing her offspring. Soon, he knew, the hatchlings would leave the nest, knowing instinctively when they were ready to be out on their own. Knowing they would not be cared for anymore.

The wind blew cold and harsh, buffeting about Hal, swirling madly in the treetops. A black, bloated cloud blotted out the sun.

Hal would be like these birds, he'd decided. He would flex his wings and fly away.

Smiling, Hal pulled the trigger.

And the sparrow fell.

Volume 3 Issue 4

"Step this way as our tour of Earth continues."

Dick Brown

Atlas

"Step this way as our tour of Earth continues."

Chalise giggled. "Get real, Atlas."

Atlas reached for Chalise's hand. "Come on, Baby," he said in that singsong voice that talked her into going out with him in the first place. "Let's go back to the bedroom, and I'll give you the rest of the tour."

Maybe it was the wine. Maybe it was the fact Atlas was already shirtless. Whatever it was, Chalise allowed him to lead her back to the bedroom.

Atlas sat her down on the bed and took a step back. He slipped off his shoes and undid his belt. Chalise kept her eyes up, studying his face—his broad brown nose, brown eyes, and his short brown hair, died bright white like the polar ice cap.

Atlas flexed his arms across his chest and kissed his biceps. "These are my Rocks of Gibraltar," he said.

"Oh, really?" Chalise asked, nodding.

Atlas loved his body. Chalise watched him for the past few months go in and out of the gym next to the laundry mat where she worked. She thought he was just another mindless body builder who spent every waking hour pumping iron. It turned out, Atlas worked there, and when he brought his laundry in one day, he and Chalise started talking. Well, Atlas talked; Chalise just listened.

Atlas was different. He was charming and funny. And smart. Well, more intelligent than some of the other guys Chalise had gone out with.

Atlas drew his arms back to reveal a wide chest and rippling abs.

"Where are we now?" Chalise asked.

"The Rocky Mountains," Atlas said, making his pecs dance. He rolled his abs. "Ever ride the rapids on the Mighty Colorado?"

Chalise smiled and shook her head. "What do you call your belly button?"

Atlas looked down, frowning, as if he hadn't ever considered the tiny indentation in his belly. "The Grand Canyon?" he said shrugging.

Chalise laughed.

Atlas looked up and smiled.

"Where to next?" Chalise asked, half-joking, trying to hide her mounting excitement.

"I'm glad you asked." Atlas unbuttoned his pants and let them fall to the floor. "You know why I call these bad boys the Great Wall of China? Because they're long and strong."

Chalise rolled her eyes, but she was clearly enjoying the tour.

Atlas slipped his thumbs under the waistband of his boxers. Chalise's grin grew into a full-blown smile, but her gaze never wavered from his.

Slowly, Atlas lowered his hands. In the periphery of her vision, Chalise could tell the boxers were on their way to join the pants on the floor.

Chalise nonchalantly lowered her eyes. She tried at once to hide her embarrassment and delight.

"What's that?" she asked, smiling. "The Eiffel Tower? No, wait." She cocked her head to the side. "The Leaning Tower of Pisa."

Atlas' smile was devilish. "No, Baby. This is Heaven on Earth."

Dale Thomas Smith

Earth Follies

"Step this way as our tour of Earth continues." The woman in the globe suit pointed to the left. Her floppy white hat had a tiny flag stuck on the beanie that was supposed to symbolize the North Pole, Johnny guessed. A wire extended from the top of the hat to about two feet above her head. On the end of the wire sat the moon. It was all very cheesy, but Johnny could hardly say no to his new girlfriend, Kandy, when she won two tickets for a behind-the-scenes tour of the brand new circus, Earth Follies. Johnny actually tried to back out, but Kandy was so damn cute, with her bobbed blond hair, slightly pugged nose, and the most adorable dimples you'd ever seen. She was a lot prettier than the others he'd dated. He could not say no to her. Plus, what were the chances of running into anyone he knew? There were a lot of carnival/circus type extravaganzas in this country.

"To the left, are the elephants of the Sahara." Sure enough, several elephants stood about in a bunch of sand. Not much of a desert, but what's a traveling circus going to do? Johnny and Kandy had already seen the Amazon, the Galapagos, and the Outback. Strange setting for a circus, but Johnny knew a gimmick was important. He was looking forward to the Great Wall of China when he heard a familiar voice. Uh oh.

"Johnny, is that you? Oh my God, I can't believe it's you!" Johnny and Kandy turned to the owner of the voice, a large woman with a long beard. The Bearded Lady. Every circus had one. She was about Johnny's height at six feet tall, but probably doubled Johnny's weight. Johnny was skinny. The Bearded Lady was not.

The Bearded Lady walked up to Johnny grinning from ear to ear, probably. It was hard to see through the beard, but she was obviously happy. She grabbed Johnny and gave him a bear hug. Kandy looked on with morbid curiosity. How did her new boyfriend know the Bearded Lady?

"I haven't seen you since we were dating," the Bearded Lady said. Kandy gasped. Johnny's face quickly turned red and he looked at Kandy with an 'I can explain' look. "How've you been?" the Bearded Lady asked.

"Uh…okay," Johnny answered. The Bearded Lady talked a while longer. Johnny was mortified. Kandy was mortified. When the Bearded Lady walked away, Johnny tried to explain.

"I was young. I didn't know what I was doing."

"When did you break up with her?"

"Well, she broke up with me. Six months ago."

Kandy stomped her foot and pouted. "Oh my God! A bearded lady? Johnny, how could you?"

Johnny and Kandy sat on Mt. Everest while Johnny pleaded and begged. After ten minutes of this, and with Kandy's tears all dried up, Kandy said she'd try to get past the fact that Johnny had recently dated a circus freak. The Bearded Lady, no less. This relationship was too important to throw away because of dumb decisions made in the past. They left Mt. Everest to try to catch up with their tour group.

A familiar voice came from behind. "Johnny, is that you? Oh my God, I can't believe it's you!" Johnny and Kathy turned to the voice. It came from down low, but was very gruff. A redheaded midget came running up. He, also, was very happy to see Johnny.

"Oh shit," Johnny said. He turned to Kandy. "I was young…"

Melissa Mead

Worlds Apart

"Step this way as our tour of Earth continues." Mr. Martin said that every year.

Mr. Martin, Ellen's neighbor, sold supplies for Willow Corners Landscaping. Every year, he'd don his green face paint and wobbly coat hanger antennae and take Willow Corners Farm and Garden fairgoers on his "Tour of Earth."

"Marble chips! We'd give our third lung for those back on Mars," he'd exclaim. Or: "Look at this potting soil! Much richer than our red stuff."

On Ellen's fifth birthday, her parents made her her own antennae and brought her to see Mr. Martin. He christened her "the Moon Baby." She gleefully dug craters in a pile of sand while customers applauded. Ellen was hooked. By age sixteen, she had an after school job with the landscaper, and fairgoers called her "Mr. Martin's Little Star." She never missed a fair.

By Ellen's first year of college, things changed. Ellen met Josh Stewart. Handsome, popular Josh drove a new red sports car. To Ellen's astonishment, he took her out in it, to dinner at Maison Mignon.

"Mr. Martin's right," Ellen sighed, sniffing her orchid corsage. "I do feel like a star tonight."

"Who's Mr. Martin?"

"Come to the fair next week! I'll introduce you."

Ellen feared Josh wouldn't come. He did. He parked the red car far from the mud-spattered farm wagons and picked his way through the rutted paths, wrinkling his nose. "This place smells like…"

"Manure," Ellen confirmed. "From the horse barns. And hay, cotton candy, and," she sniffed, "Mrs. Gunnerson's blueberry turnovers. I'll get two. Then we'll go see Mr. Martin."

Ellen soon lost sight of Josh in the bustle—especially after Mrs. Gunnerson spotted her, caught her up in a rib-crushing hug, and peppered her with questions about her parents, her classes, and the exorbitant price of canning jars these days. Ellen finally tore herself free, bought the turnovers, and found Josh, waving to her over the crowd and laughing.

"Come see the scarecrow!" he called.

Scarecrow? Were the kids having a contest? Ellen picked her way through the crowd to Josh's side.

"Look at that old geezer! I thought only patients in bad psych-ward movies wore tinfoil hats." He pointed.

It was Mr. Martin. His latest costume was all tinfoil, with red and blue stars pasted on.

"Step this way as...Little Star! Come give an old spaceman a hand!"

"Not today, Mr. Martin," Ellen murmured.

"I see—got a beau with you. He can help. C'mon up, son!"

"He's nuts!" Josh hissed.

"No! It's...fun. Really. C'mon."

"You're the nut." Josh marched off. Mr. Martin hurried over.

"I didn't mean to embarrass your young man, Ellen. Go after him."

"Your audience is waiting," Ellen muttered, sprinting for the parking lot.

Half an hour later, Ellen passed Mrs. Gunnerson's booth again. "Want a cider doughnut, hon? What's in the bag?" the old woman bellowed.

"No thanks. I've got to deliver this before it wilts."

"Ah, flowers for your boyfriend?" Mrs. Gunnerson winked knowingly. "Handsome young devil. I'm not sure he's the type to let the girl give him flowers, though."

Ellen didn't reply. She made her way back to the landscaping booth where Mr. Martin still held forth on the wonders of Earth's potting soil. He looked older, tired. Much more wilted than Ellen's primrose and pink Star Rosebush.

She stepped forward, holding out the plant. Mr. Martin looked up, puzzled.

"I bring a gift from the people of Earth to the Galactic Ambassador," Ellen intoned.

Mr. Martin stepped down, gravely accepting the "tribute." Only Ellen heard the quaver in his voice. "Thanks, Little Star."

Volume 3 Issue 5

"Please state your name for the court."

Jeff Adams
Television Trials

"Please state your name for the court." The TV blares that out for the third time today, and I can't take it anymore.

"Can't you find something else to watch?" I shout—too loudly—across the dorm room at my roommate who has himself planted squarely in front of the television. In the two weeks we've lived together, I'm still not used to this afternoon ritual. It starts at noon with two, yes two, episodes of *Judge Judy*, then an hour later it's off to a different channel for *Divorce Court*, then he's popping between channels for the next half hour between ancient *People's Court* reruns on some cable channel and something called *Power of Attorney* on another. The next hour of TV's okay because he picks up a rerun of *Law and Order*, so at least there's a decent plot. But right after that, it's off to *Judge Mills Lane*, and somehow he squeezes in a couple more *Divorce Courts*, or maybe it's *People's Court?* I get confused.

Today's really bad because my afternoon class was cancelled, so I'm home when I'm not usually here. That means a full-out assault today. I've asked him why he does this; don't think I haven't. He says it's law school prep. I haven't seen that on any pre-law requirements at the school. After the first week of living with him, I looked into it. Thought he might be tellin' me the truth. He's not. I don't even think they're real lawyers on those shows, so I don't see what good it could do.

I've considered knocking the TV out of the window. Not sure what he would do if I did that. It's close enough to the window that it could look like an accident if I did it just right. Course, if there's someone outside and it hits them, I could end up on one of those stupid shows. I think it would be self-defense or temporary insanity though. I bet I'd get on *Law and Order* with that sort of case. I can hear the promo: "Ripped from the headlines…college freshman goes insane and throws TV out of the window, killing his classmates…But is he insane or was it murder? Don't miss the last five minutes for a *Law and Order* twist you've got to see to believe. *Dawson's Creek*'s Kerr Smith guest stars in an all-new *Law and Order*, part of must-see Wednesday on NBC."

Okay, I've got an overactive imagination. Not only do I go for the entire NBC dialogue with that, I even get myself played by a hunky dude whose only resemblance to me is black hair. My fantasy, so why not, right? A boy can dream after all. If I have to become a tragedy of the week, I might as well look good doing it. Of course, Kerr might not be able to do it, not sure if the WB has rules about guest starring against your own network's show. I'll have to work on alternate casting.

At least the time's almost up. When it's over, he heads out for dinner and he's not back until near midnight when there's one last *Judge Judy* on. At least he plugs in his headphones for that, and if I'm lucky, I can sleep through the flicker.

I hear the final verdict coming; he's already puttin' his shoes on. Woo hoo. I gotta nuke some popcorn and hop on the bed, it's almost time for *Oprah* and then *Ricki* and *Rosie*, and there's just time for *Ilyana* before dinner.

Jennifer Schwabach

Queen for a Day

"Please state your name for the court." The seneschal sounded bored. Well he might. She was the twenty-seventh woman in as many weeks to take the King's Challenge.

Dotty threw back her head. "Dorthea Penelope Clementina Helena Temer-Whithenstein." Most of that had been added by the Village Council, who agreed that "Dotty the Shepherdess" didn't sound very impressive.

The seneschal droned back, "Do you understand that you will be permitted to reign as Queen of Westerlake for a period of one day, after which, your performance will be evaluated for suitability to take up the position permanently?"

"I do."

"And you further understand that if you are judged suitable, you will be expected to take up the scepter of the Queen of Westerlake and all the duties and privileges therein?"

"I do," Dotty repeated. She had made it a point to sit in the gallery for the last three Challenges. She'd read up on as many historical cases as she could. It had been over a century since a Queen of Westerlake had died without female issue.

Dotty glanced around the court. Well-dressed women stood around, their husbands beside them. Today, the men, too, would have input into the court proceedings.

King Vernon cleared his throat. Perched on his mother's throne, the late Queen's only child looked like a child still, though Dotty knew him to be past twenty. "You may come and join me upon the throne."

Ascending the steps, she seated herself next to him. Would he make a good husband? Did it matter?

She watched the incoming supplicants calmly. She knew, from the last three challenges, that the difficulty would most likely come from one of them. The first man begged that one of the royal physicians take a look at his daughter. The girl had fallen, and would not wake. None of the healers could help her. Dotty nodded, waved a hand, and the man was led off to the infirmary. Surely that could not be the challenge?

Next came a man who asked permission to wed his son into the House of Derryquar. "Do your son and the Heir love each other?"

"They do, My Queen."

When you bred sheep too much, they became sickly and stupid. She'd heard that other countries had unhealthy royalty because they interbred too much. She nodded. "New blood may do the House good. They may wed." Bowing, the man left. Again, that could not have been the challenge. A cry of fear startled her eyes upward. A young girl hung from the bunting of the balcony, dangling over the two-story drop. Jumping to her feet, Dotty pushed Vernon aside and seized an armload of cushions from the throne. She ran and placed them under the girl. Seeing what she was doing, Vernon followed suit. Dotty raced back and pulled the huge banner from behind the throne. "Take a corner!" She yelled to Vernon. She nodded to the seneschal to do the same. A woman joined them to take the fourth corner. Moving over the pile of cushions, she called to the girl, "Let go! We'll catch you!"

The girl, after a moment's hesitation, dropped into the center of the banner, which dipped with the sudden weight. The cushions protected her from serious injury.

The rest of the day passed uneventfully.

As the last petitioner filed out, she said, "Did I pass, Sir?"

"Oh, before lunch," Vernon grinned. "You showed yourself to be compassionate, wise, and able to think quickly in a crisis." There had been three challenges, after all. "So, My Queen, what is your name when you're not at court?"

"Dotty," Dotty admitted.

Simon Wood

Your Name, Please

"Please state your name for the court."

"I'd rather not say."

"I don't care what you'd rather," the prosecutor hissed. "This is a court of law, and you've been accused of willful assault. You are bound by law to answer my questions. Now state your name for the court."

It was inevitable. He was tired of keeping the secret. He'd gotten away with it for so long, but he knew, eventually, someone would force him to tell. Well, it might as well be today.

"Omega," he replied soulfully. "Undoer of worlds, the end of all things."

"At last. It's better than the John Doe I have down here." The prosecutor tapped his clipboard. "Omega." The prosecutor chewed the word over.

In the distance, a storm voiced its disapproval.

Omega sighed.

"And that's really your name?"

Omega nodded.

"That's an interesting name. Where did it come from?"

"It was the name I was given after my trial."

The prosecutor sneered. "So, you've been in trouble with the law before. Would you like to elaborate?"

"I loved a God. I, as a mortal, wasn't worthy. But she still allowed me to love her. We were caught and exposed, and I was condemned for an eternity."

The prosecutor hid a smirk behind his hand. Members of the gallery and jury exchanged childish grins or confused shrugs. Omega's defender closed his eyes and shook his head. The judge rose above the theatrics and cleared his throat.

The storm gathered pace. Thunder rumbled and rain pelted the courthouse windows.

"So, you're expecting this court to believe that?"

"Yes."

"Interesting." The prosecutor reviewed his notes. "This seems to reflect a similar conversation you had with the plaintive, Hector Gomez."

"Yes."

"Just before you hit him." The prosecutor had to shout to be heard over the hailstones rat-a-tat-tatting off the courthouse roof.

"Yes."

"Breaking his jaw in two places."

"I wouldn't know."

"Well, I would. I have his medical chart in front of me." The prosecutor returned his notes to his desk. "Why did you hit Mr. Gomez?"

"To prevent him from undoing the world."

"Because that's your job, right?" Lightning flashed, filling the courtroom with blinding light.

Omega shook his head. "Not my job, my burden."

"That's good of you to take on such a demanding role." The prosecutor smirked at the jury. His humor was shared.

"It's not a role I wish to have or wish on anyone else."

The prosecutor leaned on the witness box. "Explain to me, exactly how do you undo a world, Omega?"

"All you have to do is say my name."

A thunderbolt rocked the courthouse.

Volume 3 Issue 6

"How did you end up with
a nickname like that?"

Margaret B. Davidson

An Arrangement of Convenience

"How did you end up with a nickname like that? Lulubelle doesn't suit you at all."

Edmond received no answer. Louise had retreated into one of her 'states.' He called them 'states of reverie' for he could think of no better term to describe the condition of preoccupation into which Louise would occasionally lapse. He knew only that afterwards she would have no remembrance at all of where her ruminations had taken her—at least no remembrance that she was willing to share with her husband. Still, he thought, it gave a fellow time with his own thoughts. Didn't want a woman who constantly chattered, did he? Now, whilst she was suitably distracted, he took the opportunity to study the colorful scene displayed before him. The surroundings were indeed exotic for one who had barely ventured from the Kansas farmlands except for one brief trip to Massachusetts—a trip that proved fortuitous when he met Louise.

Edmond had often dreamed of Paris but had never anticipated actually being there. This café on the Champs-Elysees was exactly as he had imagined it would be—bubbling with life and laughter; the mix of people was eclectic but ever elegant, to his hungry eyes at least. He mentally hugged himself in satisfaction and congratulation that he had succeeded in causing his prospects to change so much for the better. His gaze turned once more to his wife of one week.

She wasn't an ugly woman. Her face was devoid of the artifice of rouge or other like adornments that women sometimes used to enhance their looks. Yes, she was plain of face, but she carried herself with a quiet elegance that was doubtless the product of good breeding. With a more stylish wardrobe, she might even pass for chic. *Perhaps this marriage won't be so bad after all.* Louise startled him from his contemplation.

"Why are you staring at me, Edmond?" Her voice and expression could not have been sweeter.

"I was merely admiring your beauty, my love. I am the luckiest man alive."

Her sweetness of expression faded ever so slightly as she arched her eyebrows and pondered a moment.

Then, "Edmond, I believe the time has come for us to be honest in our expectations of one another. You did not marry me for love, nor even for a slight fondness…"

"That's not true…"

"…for a slight fondness of anything but gaining a better station in life."

"I…"

"Prey, let me continue. I have long been aware of your motivation, and I find no fault with it. I am no longer a young woman, and my own options were somewhat limited. This union we have formed will work for the benefit of us both. You have gained access to my wealth and I, in turn, have gained a husband that will allow me to conduct the kind of social life I have long craved, a life that would have been impossible for me had I not drastically changed my own circumstances."

"My love, you do me a grave injustice."

Louise's smile was wry as she again ignored Edmond's protestation.

"You asked about my nickname. You asked about Lulubelle."

Edmond was most relieved at the change of subject.

"Yes, I heard somebody address you that way once. An old acquaintance of yours, I believe."

"They called me that in the house."

"What?" He looked blank. "What house are you talking about?"

"The house—my place of business."

"Huh?" He must be misunderstanding. Then his face cleared and he chuckled as he realized that his wife was joking. She was proving full of surprises. He had never taken her as a person having much in the way of a sense of humor.

"Where did you imagine my fortune came from, Edmond? I don't recall introducing you to a plethora of well-placed relatives." Her smile was enigmatic.

"But, Louise…" Edmond, for once, was lost for words. Who was this woman he had married?

He studied her unremarkable features looking for an answer but finding none. Then, as full understanding of what she had told him at last hit home, he grinned. He grinned slowly at first, but then that grin became wider and wider until it lit up the whole of his handsome face. "Oh my Lord," he spluttered.

"Darling, do be quiet; people are looking." Louise's grin was hidden as she took a seemly sip from her wineglass.

T.K. Harris
The Nickname

"How did you end up with a nickname like that?"

Chubby glanced down at his stick-like arms and shrugged. "I don't know. Guess it's kind a like the tall guy being called, Tiny, or the fat guy, Slim." Chubby looked across the table at his cellmate who had resumed eating. The guy was the embodiment of the movie prisoner. Muscular, dark featured, and smelly. "So what about you?"

"What about me?" he asked, spewing his food.

"How'd you get your nickname?"

His cellmate smiled, showing nicotine-stained teeth. "You mean, Jerry The Eyes?" He laughed quietly for a minute before leaning across the table, placing two large tattooed arms on either side of his food tray. "It's 'cause I like to take my victim's eyes. I'd just sort of scoop 'em out like this." He made a motion with his spoon, and Chubby paled. "You know, you got kind of pretty eyes."

Chubby jumped out of his seat. "Hey, man. What's going on? They said this wasn't maximum security. All I did was steal some TVs!"

The inmates around him were laughing now, including his cellmate. A guard motioned for Chubby to take a seat, which he did reluctantly.

Jerry smiled at him. "Just kidding, Chubby."

Chubby eyed him suspiciously. "Man, what you did—that's not funny."

Jerry rolled his eyes, and then leaned a little closer and whispered. "Okay. Okay. Look, the truth is I got the nickname when I was a kid and had to wear glasses." Jerry plunged his spoon into the gelatin mess that passed for dessert and stuffed it into his mouth.

Chubby looked at him for a moment, before turning back to his food. "That still wasn't funny."

Jerry The Eyes was still laughing as they filed back to their cells, one hand clutched tight around the spoon he'd stuck in his sleeve.

G.W. Thomas

Lazarus

"How did you end up with a nickname like that?"

"Lazarus? Well, there's a story behind that," I tell them. The three old men nod. They know the form, even if kids these days don't. They still remember how to listen.

"I used to work in a funeral home," I begin. "Martin's Funeral Chapel. 'Best Coffins This Side of Topeka.'"

The old men nod again, but they start to eye the coffeepot on the stove.

"I've also suffered from narcolepsy since I was five. I was struck on the head by a warm bottle of milk. Since then, when I get too excited, I fall asleep."

The old men grin. They can sense a story now. I have them back.

"It happened when I was preparing a coffin for a man who was to be displayed in only ten minutes. I bent over the empty coffin, checking the lining, which was bunching in an unsightly way. When I saw this big spider on the coffin lid! I was startled, fell asleep instantly. I plunged into the coffin, head first and out like a light in a whorehouse."

The old toothless grins of anticipation mark my way to the finish line. "When I fell, of course, I jerked the lid, which closed tight. Jimmy, our coffin attendant (not the sharpest tool in the shed, as we say in Kansas) took the coffin out and opened it for display. I usually don't sleep too long when I've had a spell, maybe a half hour at most. It was when the dead man's aunt was saying, 'He looks so natural, so peaceful,' that I sat up, yawning like a kitten."

Chuckles escape through old lips. Now for the kill.

"Well, we were pretty busy after that, treating six relatives for shock, a couple for wet trousers, and one case of laughter from a woman in the back who no one knew. So, that's how I got the nickname Lazarus after that guy in the Bible. I also got my pink slip."

They slapped me on the back with their appreciation. I grinned and fell over. I needed the nap anyway.

Contributors

Jeff Adams is the coeditor and cofounder of *The First Line*. By day, he is a senior producer with the admissions services division of The Princeton Review. By night, he's a writer, hockey player, and theatre goer. He lives in New York City with his partner, Will.

Nick Aires is a recent finalist in the L. Ron Hubbard Writers of the Future contest, and he has published over 30 stories in anthologies such as *Enchanted Realms II*, magazines such as *Amazing Journeys*, ezines such as *Planet Relish*, and on Story House coffee can labels. He is also the coeditor of *Fantasy Readers Wanted—Apply Within* from Silver Lake Publishing. Readers can contact him at nickaires@yahoo.com.

Joe Austin works in the publishing industry. He earned a master's degree in creative writing from CUNY Queens College in December, 2000 and lives in Queens, NY with his partner, Rick, and their dog, Billy.

Jennifer Bass lives in Cincinnati, Ohio, where she's forever studying Japanese history and literature. In addition, her dream of hugging a panda continues to persist.

Josh Beddingfield is a political editorialist, finish carpenter, and Subaru mechanic in Bend, Oregon. He is at work on a long story about arson in the eastern Oregon woods.

Dick Brown bench pressed 127 pounds once. However, that is the extent of his weightlifting knowledge.

Harold Brown has written many stories, but published very little. He's hoping his extensive comic book collection will support him, if his writing never does.

Chris Buchan lives in Columbus, Ohio, with his beautiful wife, Heather, and children, Raylynn and David. He spends most of his time working by night and, by day, raising kids, preparing for the arrival of the next Buchan addition, and of course, writing.

Tracie Clayton's writing made its debut in *The First Line*. She is currently finishing work on a contemporary women's novel.

Kristine Coblentz fits writing and other creative ventures in the quiet spaces between family, friends, and travel. Constructive responses welcome at kpcsmail@yahoo.com.

Kathleen Crow is a writer who lives and works in Kansas City. She has written several short stories, has had a play produced, and is currently working on a screenplay.

Margaret B. Davidson was born and raised in England. She now lives in upstate New York with her husband and cat. Margaret's husband lends moral support to her writing endeavors, while the cat helps with the typing.

Hester Eastman is a frustrated administrative assistant who reads through her bosses' mail during the day and enjoys making people uncomfortable in public at night.

Lisa Firke grew up in Princeton, New Jersey, which is said to account for her bookworm-geek chic. She now lives with her husband, children, and dogs at a boarding school in Connecticut. Look for her on the Web at www.hitthosekeys.com, where she encourages other writers to overcome writer's block.

Recently married, **Miranda Garza** and her husband live in a small town called Benchley, just outside of Bryan, Texas. They are expecting their first child. She writes: "Writing has been a part of me since I could hold a pen, and I hope our child develops the same love for writing as I have."

Theo Glenn is a writer living in Texas with his wife and two kids.

T. K. Harris is a programmer by day and a writer whenever life allows. Harris has been published in various magazines including *FMAM*, *Story House*, and *The First Line*, along with being published on www.mysterynet.com, and in two poetry anthologies. Harris currently writes stories in several genres, and the occasional article.

Joseph Horne writes and lives in Atlanta, Georgia. He can be reached at seasonalthought@yahoo.com.

Larry M. Keeton is a retired Army officer who now works for a county in Washington State. He enjoys writing, especially mystery and suspense.

Michael Kelly's fiction has appeared in a number of magazines and anthologies, including *Flesh & Blood*, *Northern Horror*, *Space & Time*, *Twilight Showcase*, and the forthcoming Cemetery Dance publication, *The HWA Presents: Dark Arts*. He is a fiction editor at *The Chiaroscuro* and edited the well-received anthology, *Songs from Dead Singers* (Catalyst Press, 2002). A collection of his short fiction, *Melancholy Rain*, will appear shortly.

After studying English literature and creative writing in college and then spending ten years in the business world, **Lara Kenney** has recently taken a break from her career in order to explore her writing full-time. Lara and her husband, Rick, live in their hometown of Pittsburgh, Pennsylvania.

David LaBounty is a children's playwright and author. He lives in Texas and is the coeditor and publisher of *The First Line*.

Mary Kay Lane lives in St. Louis, Missouri. She is a library assistant and writes short fiction and poetry.

Although mostly from southern Idaho, **Ben Lareau** has spent a great deal of time living in Massachusetts and Utah. At the moment, he lives in Maine with his wife, Christina, and their two cats. He plans to start writing a novel sometime soon.

Walter Addison March works with computers and lives with his wife and two cats. He'd rather work and live with his wife and two cats and play with his computer, but we can't have everything, can we?

From his home in southeastern Massachusetts, **W. Eric Martin** writes about games, books, technology, and cooking oil. He is working on a series of stories about wishes, and you can participate by sending your wishes to him at eric@cluestick.org.

Joshua McDonald can't believe he's in this anthology! A three-time contributor to *The First Line*, he is a writer looking for a break in NYC.

Joy L. McDowell is a graduate of the University of Oregon. She works from her studio on the edge of the Coos Bay Estuary along the southern Oregon Coast. Her essays, poetry, and short stories have appeared in publications in Oregon, New York, and Texas.

Melissa Mead sold her first short story to *The First Line* in 1999. Her most recent sale was to *Parageography*.

Matt Miller lives in Chicago where he has worked as a freelance journalist, night life reviewer, essayist and is an all-around swell guy. He is best known for writing crap for "The Sheckey's Guide Chicago," garbage for the "Chicago Voice," and a pack of lies for "Newcity." He has had countless correspondences with the producers of NPR's "This American Life" for pieces that would never be produced and is the author of three and a half novels that, to this day, are sitting on the floor in his closet waiting to be discovered. *TFL* was his very first publication and he his proud to be included in this anthology.

Sharon O'Hara lives and works in Oregon, accompanied by a husband of long standing and the occasional small mammal.

Kim Perrone writes parenting and health and human interest articles for various publications. Her true writing passion is fiction, and she has several short stories, as well as a young adult novel, in the works. Two children under the age of five and mugs of coffee at 9 p.m. are her inspirations.

Ehren Hemet Pflugfelder is currently a student and teaching assistant at Case Western Reserve University and is working on his masters in English Literature with a focus on literary theory and the Twentieth Century novel form. He loves independent movies and music, is usually writing something, and has recently completed a chapbook collaboration. He is also the author of two unnecessarily confusing and needlessly violent novels.

Ed Phelts is a computer software engineer who enjoys writing short stories and novels. His latest of three self-published novels is *Hunter and Ashby* (visit www.buybooksontheweb.com). He lives in Elkins Park, Pennsylvania.

Chris Salter is a happily married professional software developer in Ottawa. In his spare time, he likes to learn more about cars and high-performance racing engines, much to his wife's dismay.

Jennifer Schwabach lives in upstate New York. Her short fiction has appeared in *The First Line* and several other publications. When she is not writing, she works as a vocational counselor for disabled veterans.

Dale Thomas Smith is a lawyer living in Kansas City, Missouri, with his wife, their son, and their two cats and one dog. His short fiction has been published in *3 A.M. Magazine*, *The Green Tricycle*, *Stick Your Neck Out*, *The Murder Hole*, and *Writers Hood*. When he grows up, he hopes to be a writer, actor, forensic pathologist, or lead singer in a rock band.

Bruce Standley is a professional chef and food service director for a school district. He stays busy with the local community theater, both on and off stage. He has one wife and three children, who live with him in Summerhill, Pennsylvania.

John Tennel would like to be remembered as a man without a past.

G. W. Thomas lives in the Cariboo region of British Columbia. His work has appeared in over 350 books, ezines, and magazines. His paperback, *The Book of the Black Sun* is available from Double Dragon. He is the senior editor and copublisher of Cyper-Pulp (http://come.to/cyberpulp).

E. Catherine Tobler makes her living as a nanny in Colorado. Her short fiction has appeared in *Jackhammer, Would That It Were, Strange New Worlds*, and *Mota*.

Clifford Turner is a native of Decatur, Georgia. He has a Bachelor or Arts in Journalism and has made his living as a stand-up comic since 1983. He resides in Myrtle Beach, South Carolina, with his wife and two kids.

Greg Wahl has had short stories published in a variety of literary magazines and a short story anthology. He lives in central Illinois where he maintains a dental practice. He and his wife Carole are the parents of six children and the proud grandparents of five grandsons and a granddaughter, Little Miss B.

Kelli A. Wilkins has written four novels and has had short stories published in numerous magazines. She recently won Second Place in the short story contest at the 2003 Philadelphia Writer's Conference and won First Place in the Weird Tales World Horror Con contest.

Spencer Williams is a native of Texas, and his contribution represents his first publication. He has recently completed a Doctorate in Toxicology at Texas A&M University and plans to continue research at the University of Michigan. He continues to write, but has started to set his words to country music instead of print.

When not with her family, immediate or extended, **Mari Whyte** acts as charge nurse at a psychiatric facility where she is thought of as a cross between Nurse Rachet and Mary Poppins.

Simon Wood is a California transplant from England. In the last three years, he's had eighty stories and articles published. His debut novel, *Accidents Waiting to Happen*, was nominated for a Bloody Dagger Award. His latest book is *Dragged into Darkness*. Learn more about Simon at www.simonwood.net.

Richard Lee Zuras' work has appeared or is forthcoming in *The Laurel Review, Weber Studies, Passages North, Confrontation, South Dakota Review, Xavier Review, Lake Effect, Big Muddy,* and *Yemassee*. He is assistant professor of creative writing at the University of Maine at Presque Isle. Currently, Richard is starting his first novel and marketing his collection of stories entitled, *Your Father and Mine*.